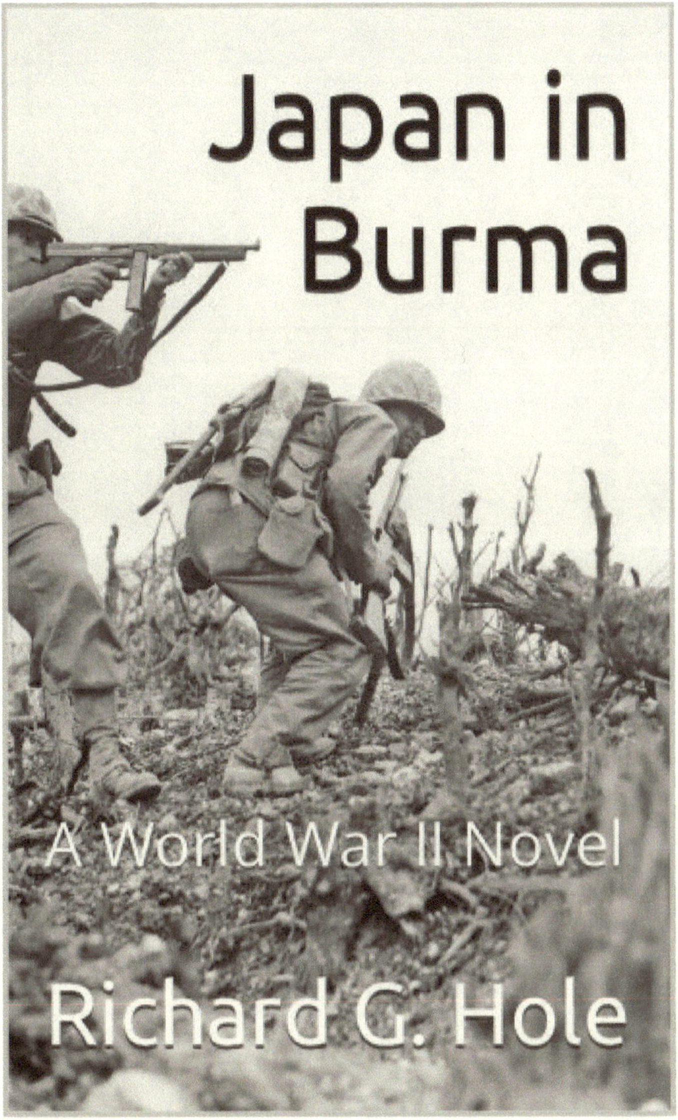

Japan in Burma

A World War II Novel

Richard G. Hole

Japan in Burma
A World War II Novel

Richard G. Hole

World War II

SYNOPSIS

The Japanese feel safe and confident.

They are advancing on almost every front in Asia and it is only a matter of a very short time before they own all of Burma.

The road to India seems to be opening up for them, only they will still have to overcome some difficulties ...

Japan in Burma is a story belonging to the World War II collection, a series of war novels developed in World War II.

JAPAN IN BURMA

I

This is Assam, in India.

It is part of the AVG. That is, "American Volunteer Group", under the command of General Chennault. We are fighting the Japanese in Burma, transporting material for the Chinese Army.

The Burma highway has fallen, but this other airway remains open, where aviation gasoline circulates that should have come from Yenanyaung in the interior of Burma; ammunition from Rangoon, clothes, food and men from America.

Because it is the vital artery that feeds the AVG of Chennault, under the supreme command of Generalissimo Chiang-Kai-Chek.

For me, it is a boring job. The only difference between an air transport unit and a group of trucks is that they go overland and you fly. Otherwise it is the same.

This was not my goal in coming here. Kunming, on the Yunnan Plateau, where the group of "Flying Tigers" was, that was my goal. A place where Japanese could be killed on a daily basis. A place where I could collect the debt that had brought me to the Far East.

Tomorrow, however, things will be better for me. Colonel Scott, who has joined the group, has obtained a hunting apparatus to protect the convoys.

And I've got another one. Tomorrow I will try it.

But this will be tomorrow. Now I just have to worry about driving this jeep down the battered road and reaching Sibsagar before the rain starts to fall. I am invited to a small party and I would be upset if something prevented me from being punctual.

Fortunately, the rain doesn't start until I get to Sibsagar. I safely reach Mohammed Azher-Khan's "bungalow" and an Indian in a white turban takes over the car.

Mohammed Azher-Khan is a brigadier in the Indian Army and he usually gives these little parties. I greet you briefly and leave my contribution on the table prepared for that purpose; It's a bottle of "whiskey," straight from Kentucky.

Mohammed, as a Mohammedan, does not drink wine, but the strongest drinks are often tasted from time to time.

Suddenly, once I am among the guests, I find that I am not attracted to being part of the meeting. It just doesn't amuse me.

The rain has stopped again; I pour myself a helping of whiskey and, glass in hand, glide into the garden. I go through the plants, mainly palm trees of various species; I sit on a stone bench, still wet, and think.

The Japanese are there, behind the Naga Hills, advancing towards India. They are yellow dwarves who have made death an institution; they say they are not afraid of it. I reason that if you do not fear death, you must ignore fear. The fact that they are already so close shows that they are tough as steel.

Will we AVG Americans rise to the occasion? Will fear appear in our ranks?

It is the great doubt. The "Flying Tigers" are making a great campaign. They are men of a special temper. I aspire to be one of them. And, again, there is the doubt right there, next to me.

It is not a good sign. I know it very well. I drink the "whiskey" in one gulp and set the glass on the bench.

"Thoughtful, Captain? "The voice comes from the right.

I look over there. I can make out the imprecise shape of a woman, covered in the traditional Indian sari. I don't see his face, but he has a musical voice and I find myself very lonely.

I point to the bench seat.

"Come here and say something" I order him.

It's very young. He may not be more than sixteen years old. Or it may be over twenty. I don't have a very good eye for these things when it comes to people of my own race. With these exotic beings, the calculation is impossible.

He sits down and smiles.

"My name is Godda," he says.

"You can call me Frank," I smile.

It's very nice to talk to Godda. I'm glad I came to the party, if only to be in an Indian garden with this young woman of another race, under the stars of a tropical sky.

* * *

At 7.30 in the morning, according to my watch, I jump into the cockpit of the magnificent P-40E, known by the name "Kittyhawks."

I adjust the rudder pedals and fasten myself with the seat belt; then I open the ignition key and press the ignition. The engine begins to roar. The three-bladed propeller, which is eleven feet high, disappears from my sight to become a transparent circle that alters the panorama ahead.

This "Allison" engine, any of the modern high-power engines, does not need to warm up; in a few seconds I'm taxiing to the runway, ready to take off.

I line it up and give gas. Speed increases gradually. I pull the joystick and find myself in midair. I pick up the landing gear and gain altitude. I describe a curve over the trees that line the field and fly over the tea plantations, green, almost the same color as they appear on the maps.

I connect the radio to hear the information regarding the presence of enemy devices, without result at the moment. But half an hour later, a British observation post reports several unidentified aircraft.

The place is somewhere in the Naga Hills. I head over there, climbing to twenty-two thousand feet, which requires adjusting my oxygen mask.

I keep an eye on the space. It's a practice outing, but just beyond the hills there may be enemy aircraft. Practice would turn into combat patrol if I trip over it.

I realize that I have forgotten much of my skill with, fighters, probably by dint of flying with transports. Here I am alone, there is no navigator to show me the course, and no autopilot to help me follow it.

Keeping a watch on the four cardinal points, in addition to below and above my apparatus would require more than a single head or; at least more than two eyes.

The sky is cloudy, but because aviators often see it, the clouds are "below," not above.

Suddenly I see a device, to my left, somewhat lower, at eight o'clock. Instantly I spring into action, dropping onto a wing in search of the enemy.

But there is no such enemy. It is a small P-43A. I have no news about where it came from, but I get closer anyway.

"P-43! "I call on the radio." Where do you come from, boy?

"Hello, P-40! "Answers a lazy voice." I just arrived and went out for a walk. The Chinese Air Force brought this beauty back saying it was being returned to us. Apparently the tanks were leaking and were catching fire one by one. They fixed it and I offered to fly with it. I come from Pensacola, but I wasn't born there. I'm from Texas.

Well, there were two of us already.

"Nice to meet you, Texas" I replied "; I'm Frank Latimer from New York.

"Well, Frankie," he said, "let's take a look.

I start to climb again and level the apparatus at thirty thousand. This is what the altimeter shows; But it must be about seven or eight thousand feet more, corrected for temperature, air humidity, and so on.

The Naga Hills are left behind. I can make out the yellow current of the Chindwin River. Stilwell Road is not far. There must be yellow children of the rising sun around those edges, both on the ground and above.

The clouds have been left behind. The landscape below, a tangle of changing green, is only broken, from time to time, by the yellow line of a river, and there, in front, by the road, which we are already reaching.

And the panorama continues deserted. I cast a casual glance around me. I think I can make out something shiny and I don't entertain myself with inquiries. I flop onto a wing and accelerate toward the object that caught my eye.

When I get a little closer, my heart leaps in my chest. It is a Japanese observation device, with a fixed landing gear.

My first enemy!

It doesn't seem to have discovered us. I go down in a violent dive and put my finger on the button that will activate the machine guns.

Now!

The six machine guns of the 50 begin to vomit shrapnel. I see the tracers heading towards the enemy, describing a funny parable, at the same time that the speed of the device decreases due to the recoil of the powerful weapons. I'm about to land my forehead on the solid precision sight in front of me.

I have just enough time to avoid a collision with the enemy aircraft, pulling the joystick and towering over it. In a single glance, during the pull of a second, I have seen the cockpit windows fly; the Japanese has turned his head, surprised by the attack.

The sight of those red circles on the fuselage and wings of the Japanese plane fires me up. I think I'm losing my cool. The result is that the Japanese pica descends into the jungle.

I turn right and then left, trying to locate him. By the time I get it, it's about four or five miles down there, just above the treetops, a silver stain that's almost invisible.

I'm going to chase him, anyway. However, the Texas voice snaps me out of my daze:

"Attention, Frankie! We have to go home!

One look at the instrument panel convinces me of this. The fuel gauge says there is hardly any fuel left to fly two and a half hours, barely what it will take to get to the field.

I turn around and search the space. Texas is near. He meets with me. I'm furious. If he had had more serenity, if he had directed the attack better, a Japanese would be dead at this hour, pierced by the projectiles of the machine guns, crushed against the muddy soil of Burma or roasted in the air if he had managed to set fire to the plane in which he was flying. .

Immersed in these musings, I consult the map and calculate the course. With Texas glued to my tail we flew into the safe skies of Assam, cruising to save gas.

The sky is lowering below us as we approach our destination, forming a continuous grayish curtain.

Really, I don't quite realize how difficult it will be to land. That field of clouds prevents all direct visibility. I have already made blind landings, but this field in Assam, in a remote part of the border territory, lacks the advances that we have become accustomed to in the United States.

I try desperately to get in touch with the field station, hoping they will be able to guide me out of that gray hell.

To my great relief, they answer me almost immediately after making the first call:

"Listen, twenty-two" I hear. Twenty-two is my identification number, freshly painted on the side of the P-40. " There is visibility, under the cloud bank, ceiling two thousand feet. Try to go down. I repeat, visibility at two thousand feet.

"Understood" I reply. I'm going there.

Texas must know as much as I do, having heard the instructions. He'll wait for me to come down. He wishes me good luck, although he's going to need a lot himself.

I slowly lose height, making a wide circle, and dive into the clouds. I feel great apprehension. At 2,000 feet I should be below the bank, but the altimeter hits 1,600 and I'm still inside that gray curtain.

Suddenly, I step out into what the operator had called a "visibility zone." Actually, even though I'm under the cloud bank, that's like looking through frosted glass. Everything appears blurry, because of the tremendous sheet of water; the rain is indescribable, a real waterfall.

Below, instead of the crossed concrete tracks, there is a lake, its surface ruffled by the shower. But it is the field, of course; I see a figure running, splashing terribly, an operations officer with red flags, who will try to help me land.

He stops and waves the flags. He points to a point and I understand that the track has to be in the indicated direction. A glance at the fuel gauge convinces me that there is no time for mistakes; zero mark.

I turn at a very sharp angle and head into what should be the track, cutting off gas immediately. Every moment I am waiting to hear how the engine begins to cough, short of gas, but that dreaded moment does not arrive.

I actuate the control to lower the landing gear, put the flaps in position and slowly lower myself. Only the fact that the operations officer, with the water mid-leg, is there, assures me that there is land under the layer of water.

Upon touching the ground, the device is suddenly braked, beginning to rebound. P-40s are not made to sit on anything other than hard concrete; I'm about to top, but I push the joystick forward and control the situation.

In an incredibly short journey, the plane comes to a stop. I'm wet from head to toe, but it's not the rain; the cabin is almost airtight. What happens is that I have sweated more in these last minutes than if I were inside a Turkish bath.

I take off my helmet and undo my seat belt. I light a cigarette and look back and up. Texas has to show up there and I hope he's as lucky as I am.

But I don't see it until, as if it were a canoe, it lifts the water off the track, leaving a turbulent wake. He must have met the same resistance as me, but he has mastered the apparatus perfectly; in a moment he has come close to where I am and, not caring about the rain, opens the dome of the cockpit.

So I decide to do the same and we get closer to each other; two men we have never met before, but we are already friends as if we had known each other for years.

We shook hands. Texas is a guy over six feet tall, smiling, and wearing cowboy boots, despite regulations prohibiting such footwear.

"We're getting wet, Texas," I tell him.

And it is strictly true. The heavy rain drenches us in a moment.

"I already noticed, Frankie" he smiles. But noticing the rain on my back makes me feel alive, so I don't feel it. Let's go to the canteen.

We run across the field as land crews rush toward the abandoned aircraft. They have to put them under cover in the hangars and check the engines and other equipment, since an exit can be ordered at any time.

We reach the canteen and, as we go, soaked to the bone, we sit down at a table. The waiter, a short young man with long hair, comes immediately.

"What's it gonna be? Asks Texas,

"'Whiskey', I would say" I reply.

And "whiskey" is. A full bottle; and then another. We don't talk too much, among other reasons because, although friends, we haven't been face to face for ten minutes yet. On the other hand, tiredness is conquering us little by little.

When the second bottle is halfway up, we go to the camp lodge and take off our wet flight suit. There is a lot of space there.

Texas occupies an empty bunk, of the four in the room, and we go to bed immediately. I suppose Texas would be the same as me; I fell asleep before touching the pillow with my head.

Someone woke me up, shaking me by the shoulders. I laboriously opened my eyes and found myself face to face with Lieutenant Colonel Mindrum, chief of field operations.

"Listen, Latimer" he says to me ". A DC-3 has left for Burma, looking for General Stilwell, you understand?

Well, Stilwell is a British general who has supreme command of all forces in India, China, and Burma. I do understand that.

"The Japanese are advancing north and it is about saving him" continues Mindrum. We could only have one crew, but I have thought of you and we will send two aircraft. Do you have something to oppose?

I shake my head negatively. Little by little, as I fully wake up, I learn more details. With Stilwell are some military personnel from his staff and war correspondent Jack Beiden. The route they were to follow would take them from Shwedo, north of the Uyu River, to the Chindwin via Homalin. Then they would continue to Sittaung and from there on the Manipur road to Imphal.

Nothing was said about how to establish contact with the group. All that was going to be done was to load the plane with food and medicine, some weapons, and leave the rest to improvisation.

Texas, who was already awake by then, smiles brightly.

"I haven't piloted a transport in a long time," he says.

"You're just going to be the copilot," I warn him, as we begin to put on our flight suits.

I see Texas doesn't carry the regulation heavy automatic, caliber .45. Instead, he has a single-action 'Colt' .45 to match his boots. We all go with weapons on missions. We know that something terrible awaits us if we are forced to crash-land or parachute.

We run to the canteen to make a quick meal. In an hour we will be in flight and we must take advantage of the time.

We are finishing, when someone appears running. A ground crew sergeant named Humphries.

"You have a visitor, Captain," he tells me. " It awaits you outside.

He leaves quickly and Texas and I walk out of the canteen. There is a car outside, the image of which reflects the wet pavement. A "Rolls" from many years ago.

The rain has stopped. We approach the car and I see Godda's face. I know she is General Azher-Khan's niece, but I only know her first name.

"A bad time for the visit, Godda" I tell him. We leave in a few minutes.

I introduce her to Texas, whose name I don't know either, and notice the beautiful scarf my friend is wearing from one night stand. I praise her and she tells me that they are made in Nepal and it is a prayer scarf. I have no idea what this means.

"I give it to you" he offers me and I take it ". So you will remember me when you are up there.

I see Mindrum nervously pacing nearby, and I understand to hurry.

"Bye, Godda" I smile. We'll see each other one of these days.

He waves and we run to the transport.

"They only have three men," Mindrum tells me. " Do what you can guys.

We take our posts, the hatches and the front door close, and I start the engines, while Texas quietly chews gum.

We took off at 2.30 in the afternoon,

* * *

We are over Burma, a good three hundred miles from the northern frontier, surveying the region between the Chindwin and the Irrawady; in other words: looking for a needle in a haystack,

We have spotted some groups, small in general; They are on their way to the Northwest, but we cannot, we have no way of identifying where Stilwell may be.

We dropped some of the packages of food, clothing, and weapons on each of the groups, continuing to make S-shaped curves. We are reaching the limit of our autonomy. This means that we will have to turn around and go home.

Below, in front, the outline, with its incredible curves, of the Northern Highway is drawn.

Well, I think, this is it. We will have to return, make a new attempt or more than one and ...

"Enemy planes!

The excited voice comes to me over the intercom. He's one of the guys in the crew. The ad puts my nerves on edge. I look out the window to my left, but I don't see anything. Yet Texas yells, too loud, I think:

"'Zeros'! Are two...!

The rest of your voice is lost. The boys in the back are shooting and drowning out the other noises. This aircraft is not armed, but we do carry light machine guns and have provided them.

Something seems to tear the transport structure apart, hitting the fuselage terribly. A shadow passes so close to us that I can even clearly make out the red spot on its side.

The thick plastic cockpit windows spray out as the cockpit fills with splinters from the instrument panel and the interior frame.

Suddenly I find that the apparatus cannot be governed; hesitates and begins to lose height.

I turn on the autopilot.

"You have to jump! I yell at Texas.

He nods his head. We leave our posts at the controls and go to the rear, to warn the crew.

What we see there leaves us in awe.

There is no crew. The three men, including the navigator, have been riddled by the passing of the «Zeros». The fuselage is full of holes and gaps, where the wind sneaks in, hissing ominously.

They had removed the door to fire their small arms through it, but it was a useless gesture.

Suddenly the plane takes a dangerous lean angle, hurtling towards the ground.

I point the door to Texas. You have to launch yourself before we go into a spin and the centrifugal force pushes us against the bulkheads and keeps us there, as if glued to the metal, until the plane crashes.

Texas jumps first. Then I let myself fall, trying to get as far away from the device as possible.

I count three seconds and pull the lock of the parachute. It opens without incident. A sharp jerk, a hollow sound, and the big umbrella is over me, gently lowering me down.

I'm looking for Texas. It is not far away. I activate the straps to land as close to him as possible. We are going to need each other when we are down there, in the jungle, populated by Japanese and with a couple of pistols for every defensive weapon.

The trees, forming an impenetrable mass, are already very close.

I remember, suddenly, the machines that have brought us down. I look up and scan the space, but I don't see them. Instead, I find that our trusty transport, despite the autopilot, is making a big curve, closing in on us again.

Then, in an instant, he raises his bow and falls heavily, out of control.

It hits the ground not far from there. I don't see any flare to indicate your fire.

Then, when I least expect it, although within the most elementary logic, I hit a tree. I see myself wrapped in the foliage; the parachute harness tangles between the branches and I hang, swinging like a pendulum.

II

Texas cannot be far; It must have fallen a short distance, since we were almost together. I open my mouth to scream warning, but the thought that there may be Japanese nearby makes me give up the attempt.

Then Texas appears walking calmly. Look up and wave:

"Come down from there" he tells me. Let's take a look at the airplane. It is close and there is food and weapons there.

True, all I have to do is turn the belt disk and then hit it to be free. However, there are more than twenty feet to the muddy ground. I risk breaking my leg, which would be worse than breaking my head.

"Find a rope," I yell at him. Cut it off your parachute. Get up on the log and throw one end at me. So maybe ...

The contortions and movements that I make, together with the fact that the branch where the parachute was hung must be half broken, make it break definitively. The fabric creaks, taking in a little air that cushions the fall.

I sink up to half a leg in the mud and pull off the parachute.

We start slowly towards the place where we have seen the device fall. It must be something like a half mile, but it took us almost two hours to find him. The mud seems to suck our boots, pulling them, and each step costs an effort.

We finally found it; It hasn't caught fire, as we already suspected, but it's horribly mangled, turned into a confusing pile of junk. The front, up to the loading door, is as flattened as an accordion; but the last third of the tail has detached from the structure, so that we can easily enter.

The load, although scrambled, appears in good condition.

"We will choose clothes first," I suggest. " These flight suits are not appropriate for riding in the jungle.

"Shorts" smiles Texas ". Let's see how these come to us.

We shed our overalls and tried on infantry clothing. That is comfortable.

Then, dressed more appropriately, we reviewed the weapons. Light and deadly submachine guns will be easier to transport than rifles. Therefore, we will take two. And hand grenades. A good portion, since we do not know how long we will be without a supply.

"Attention! "Whispers Texas." There is someone outside.

I peek through the cracks in the fuselage. I don't see anyone, no matter how hard I try. Maybe it's some Texas hallucination.

Suddenly, I see something. A kind of dark tube sticking out next to a tree, the barrel of a rifle!

Texas, next to me, exclaims in a low voice:

"Japanese!

They will have seen the plane go down and they are coming to reconnoitre. It would be important to know if they have seen us. In case they don't know we're here and there aren't many, we might surprise them.

If there are twelve or fifteen Japanese and they know that we are inside, waiting, the surprise will be for us.

I pull the lever of my submachine gun to put a round in the chamber and find the steel slipping from my hand. I have them wet; A slow stream runs down your back, which should be hot, but this sweat is not due to heat.

Then, from behind the barrel, a head appears. I look at Texas and we exchange a smile. That guy is not a Japanese. His features are not Mongolian and he wears a turban. Then I seem to have made out the neck of his warrior. That is an Anglo-Indian uniform.

I've seen guys like this before.

"Gurkha" Texas tells me.

I nod. I peek through the porthole and wave my hand at him, expecting to be hit by a bullet by mistake. But none of this happens. That man is a mountaineer and must have good eyesight. He walks forward smiling, and when I turn to say something to Texas I see another gurkha, rifle and all, poking out of the shattered window on the other side.

The two of them meet us.

Will they speak English? I guess so. And I am right.

"American people? "Asks the first one we saw, a small guy, but strong as a wolf.

I nod.

"I am the sergeant ..." and he gives a name that I would not be able to repeat even if I proposed it. " Our company was annihilated along the Irawaddy, near Shwebo. Only two of us escaped.

He introduces me to his partner, taller than him, but with another impossible name.

"Little Gurkha and Big Gurkha" says Texas.

This, at least, will be clearer.

Little Gurkha scowls at me.

"Eat" he says. We are hungry.

After all, it's not a bad idea. Now that the issue is mentioned, I feel a kind of discomfort in my stomach that cannot be anything other than hunger.

I feel the expectant gaze of my companions fixed on me. I understand the reason. We all belong to the allied forces and I am the highest ranking officer; I have to take command. However, I don't know how to send men, but how to handle airplanes; but the thing has no remedy.

"Stand guard," I say to Big Gurkha. Take something to eat and climb a tree. Warn if someone is approaching.

Big Gurkha nods in salute, takes the can of preserves and dried bread I give him, and exits the wrecked plane. The rest of us prepare for food, sitting down anyway.

We eat with appetite. Fortunately, these Gurkhas are not as complicated as the Hindus when it comes to food.

We're finishing up when a low-pitched whistle sounds. Little Gurkha jumps up and goes outside. It must be the alarm signal. Texas and I grabbed our guns and lay on the floor of the plane, peering through the holes in the fuselage.

We see that Little Gurkha takes one of the trails and, with very little precaution, advances along it until he is out of sight. This amazes me. I have read somewhere that Gurkhas are excellent soldiers. I guess this one knows what he wants to do.

Then, after a quarter of an hour, we have the explanation. Big Gurkha, from his position on the tree, has seen a group of people, has identified them and passed the notice to his companion, who comes out to bring them together with us.

When the group reaches the clearing where we are, Texas and I exchange a blank look. Little Gurkha brings four more people. There is a soldier in the Chinese Army, a tall Sikh lieutenant with a turban and a beard, a European civilian, as the whites are called here; maybe six foot four inches tall with fiery red hair.

AND...

"A woman! Exclaims Texas.

His suit is in tatters and his shoes are ruined, but this does not detract from his appeal; she would have attracted attention anywhere, even dressed in a jacket.

"I guess," says Texas, "if we stay with the wreckage long enough, we can muster an army. There must be fighters from all allied units around those contours.

"And also Japanese," I observe dryly. " We must get out of here at once.

Little Gurkha agrees with me, coming quickly, after interviewing Big Gurkha.

"Japanese! "Informs" Ten men. They are coming this way. From the south.

We hurriedly get out of the plane food, clothing and weapons.

"We can set the device on fire," suggests Texas.

Shake your head negatively.

"We will station ourselves around the clearing," he ordered. They are only ten men and we can easily finish them off if we surprise them.

The Sikh lieutenant distributes the cargo we are going to carry and we run into the undergrowth at the edge of the clearing, spacing around the wrecked craft. The only thing missing is Big Gurkha, who is still perched on his tree.

There is a tense wait, during which we remain silent. We are a heterogeneous group of people who have nothing in common, who do not know each other, but who are on the same side. On the other are the Japanese, a mortal threat to all.

I see them appear suddenly at the edge of the clearing. Their bayonets are fixed and they advance leaning forward, small, silent, deadly. They don't expect to find but a few corpses, I suppose.

They cross the clearing and approach the plane, peering through the opening in the tail.

I face the submachine gun and put my finger on the trigger.

I fire the first volley, and my other teammates fire anyway.

Some Japanese fall, caught by surprise. Three or four hide in the demolished apparatus, and as many fall to the ground and answer our fire.

Our positions are better. We are covered; but these yellow dwarfs are tough to peel. They keep a blazing fire and scream bloodcurdling screams.

Then four of them go on the attack! They run towards us, their gleaming bayonets in the muzzle of their rifles, while the others cover them with their fire.

Texas pulls the ring off a grenade, holds it for a few moments, and throws it at the attackers. The explosion stirs the air. Two Japanese roll on the ground and freeze. Another tries to crawl, always ahead. The fourth, defenseless, continues with the load.

We concentrate our shots on him and see him fall only a few yards away; his face has a cruel, hideous grin that disappears behind a bloody mask in a thousandth of a second.

Texas one after another, throws more grenades. The device suddenly catches fire. The fuel tanks will have cracked in the crash of the forced landing and the pumps ignite the fuel.

Through the flames, three more Japanese appear, running like demons, in an attempt to win the forest. One of them, an officer, brandishes his samurai sword in the air.

We take them down quickly and I look around to see if we have any casualties, which fortunately hasn't happened.

I hear a few more shots. The Gurkhas are finishing off the wounded. I have a bitter taste in my mouth, but I have not been able to do anything to prevent it; after all, we are combatants and we have to put sentimentality aside.

The Sikh officer hasn't even blinked, and the woman is lighting a cigarette.

We, we all meet, forming a compact group.

"How far can we walk each day? "I ask.

The Sikh officer thinks for a moment.

"Four miles, maybe, five" he answers.

We are about four hundred miles from the border, in a country occupied by Japanese forces. Forty or fifty miles to the west the Chindwin River slides, snaking north. We must reach this current that will guide us and reach Manipur.

It will take days or months, but it is our only hope of survival.

We have provisions for a week, according to my estimate. We are well armed and we have spare clothes. If there is a bit of luck, if we glide like ghosts through the jungle and watch our steps, there are chances of getting it.

Now I notice that what I believed to be a woman is only a girl.

There is courage in her eyes, but she is only about a girl.

"What is your name? "I ask.

Doris McDonald.

"Well, Doris, try putting on a uniform and a pair of boots" I say. You have to walk hard for a long time. Let's go to the Chindwin. Then we will take the Northern route. If we stay strongly united and disciplined we can achieve it. Do you think you can follow us?

She stares at me with her big clear eyes.

"I will go as far as you go," he affirms serenely.

So, once we share the load, we get going. A tiny guerilla. A combat patrol made up of seven men of different races and one woman.

I think I'm optimistic to even think we're going to get out of this one, but we'll give it a try.

The Sikh lieutenant, with his unflappable demeanor, stands next to me.

"The rainy season is about to end," he tells me. " Two weeks, maybe three, and we will be in the dry season. Then we can go faster. We were to deploy the Gurkhas to serve as scouts for us. These people know the jungle very well.

I nod and the Sikh barks orders. He seems like a good soldier, and his nerves are top-notch. The Gurkhas stand out and disappear from our sight.

The undergrowth seems impenetrable, but there is always a hole to slide through. It is a land of trees, with lianas and foliage forming thick curtains between the trunks. There are animals, especially above, in the branches. I see birds of glistening plumage and hear the strange cries of monkeys, distinguishing a few flocks from time to time.

There are other kinds of animals too. For example, snakes; I'm about to step on one, but Doris has seen it before me and she screams warning.

The snake lifts the front and puffs it up in a curious way.

I look at her, feeling invincible disgust, not knowing what to do. The Chinese soldier finishes with her quickly. With a machete blow the part in two halves.

"A" fifteen minute "cobra" smiles the red-haired giant coldly.

"The name is curious" I comment.

"Of the most. No one is known to have lived more than a quarter of an hour after being bitten by one of these critters."

I understand that the Japanese will be just one more danger, not the only one, of those who will stalk us in the Burmese jungle. Now every time I put my foot down, I feel a strange sensation, dreading stepping on one of those nasty snakes.

I wonder if we are marching in the same direction as the two Gurkhas before us, but the Sikh lieutenant does not hesitate for a moment and I am confident that we are on the right track.

The ground is a quagmire. There is thick, dark mud where the boots stick and it is difficult to pull them with every step.

I wonder how the Gurkhas could have gone faster than us. In certain places we have to break through with machetes; it is the Chinese soldier and the Sikh lieutenant who handle them, and very cleverly, by the way.

The Sikh stops and raises his hand. We stop, preparing the weapons. The undergrowth rustles in front of us and Little Gurkha appears, his face glistening with sweat.

"Japanese! "Simply report." Half a mile from here. They are working.

"How many? "I ask.

"About fifty. They have cleared a piece of flat land and have many drums stacked under the trees.

Something hums in the sky. We cannot see it because of the treetops; but we know that it is a single-engine machine, perhaps a "Zero".

The noise increases in volume and we have a fleeting image of the enemy plane. It flies very low and, within minutes, the engine hum is suddenly lost.

I think the best thing would be to go in the opposite direction to the clearing Little Gurkha is talking about. Fifty Japanese is too many for us to do anything but flee; but I am curious to know what they are doing and I wonder about the contents of the drums that they pile up in the middle of the jungle.

"Let's go" he smiled at Little Gurkha. We'll take a look at the dwarves.

Little Gurkha smiles too. He is small in stature, but the Japanese are even smaller, and he is pleased with this, I think.

We now advance slowly, guided by the gurkha, in the direction of the clearing and we finally come across Gurkha. He is lying on the ground, and he turns his head when he hears us coming.

He points with his hand. Ahead, in an almost flat depression, the Japanese have built an airstrip. The cans by the trees, piled up carelessly, are made of aviation gasoline. They may have been parachuted, to be deposited there. For now, the "Zeros" have enough ground to land. Then, when the runway is longer, the transports can do it too.

I imagine that the Japanese are seeding the occupied territory with these small airfields, so that they allow their planes to operate close to the front line.

I remember our recent fight with the Japanese patrol. We could try something similar here. But, there are fifty ...

The "Zero" we heard earlier is there, too. He has landed and is at the edge of the clearing.

The Sikh lieutenant hands me his binoculars and I survey the place. There are three sentries patrolling around the fuel cans. Others, likewise, watch the surroundings of the field. But most of the yellows go unarmed, working like Negroes, cutting down trees and pushing them aside to clear more ground.

"Only three sentries" I observe. " We could try to surprise them as soon as night falls. Those drums will be easily pierced with a knife. The terrain slopes slightly towards the airfield. The gasoline would drop under its own weight to the track.

"It can be done," says the Sikh lieutenant. The two gurkhas and I will take care of the work. You don't go out into the open. "We will eliminate the sentries and return here, after the gasoline is running. We will let it soak the ground before turning it on. They may find out about the plan sooner from the smell. Then, likewise, we set it on fire and we will have targets very illuminated by the fire.

Simple, but risky. However, it is worth a try.

"We will try" I tell him. We are going to rest until the night.

Texas looks at his watch.

"Three hours" he says laconically.

III

The three hours last forever. The sun sets more slowly than ever before today. The darkness begins to take over the jungle.

The Japanese make a lot of noise. They have finished the day's work and will be drizzling dinner with sake, the rice liqueur. I suppose there must be more than one guerrilla operating around these contours, remnants of Indian, British or Chinese units decimated by the fighting.

However, these Japanese feel safe and confident. They are advancing on almost every front in Asia and it is only a matter of a very short time before they own all of Burma; The path of India seems to be open to them, only they will still have some difficulties to overcome.

I smile in the dark. I think that if we are going to give them all the difficulties they are going to have, the war is lost for the allies.

What do we want? I guess, save your life, reaching our lines. But everything is very confusing, at least for me. The company is desperate, do not have any illusions about it. I suppose that, not being fatalistic, we will do anything less than surrender to the Japanese.

The darkness is already complete. There is no moon. The noises of the Japanese camp are dying out, little by little, and soon a great silence reigns, broken occasionally by the thousand noises of the jungle, ghostly and strange.

The Sikh lieutenant approaches. The two Gurkhas come with him, ready to go on the adventure.

"We must eliminate the sentries," I tell them. " Then, trying not to make the least noise, pierce as many drums as possible. Immediately, come back here. If something goes wrong, win the forest and flee north. We will follow them.

That is all. The Gurkhas hold the long, curved blades of their knives between their teeth, and the Sikh does the same with his machete.

They glide, crouching like wild beasts, toward the clearing; out of sight in a second.

The wait is tense. It is disturbing to be here, in the dark, waiting for the moment to scare fifty brave Japanese soldiers, when, very well, we can be scared, as soon as things go wrong.

I consult the luminous dial of my watch. The Gurkhas and the Sikh left at 9:40. It seems to me as if time has stopped. I put the watch to my ear and convince myself that it runs normally.

Minute by minute, half an hour passes. Impatience gnaws at my guts; but I have realized that, in some way, all the members of our group have placed the responsibility on my shoulders. I can't let you down. Even if I am not, I must look like the bravest of all.

The bearded face of the Sikh lieutenant appears suddenly, barely visible in the pale starlight. The two gurkhas follow. This means that everything is going well, which fills me with satisfaction.

Now, we have to wait for the gasoline to slide into the Japanese camp. On the wet mud, with the soaked earth it gives humidity, the fuel will run easily, I think.

I would like to know the details of the task carried out by these three good soldiers; how they surprised the sentries and eliminated them without the slightest noise, accomplishing a real feat.

I stop thinking about these things when someone starts yelling down there in the Japanese camp.

I don't understand the language, but the voice can only refer to one thing. Gasoline is soaking the earth and the Japanese have noticed this, no doubt by smell.

You have to act quickly.

"The grenades! "scream". Don't waste your time!

I unlock one of them and throw it forward with all my might. Texas rolls another.

The explosion of mine raises the echoes of the forest. Then the one in Texas bursts and the stage lights up. An immense blaze breaks out, seeming to rush forward, engulfing the camp.

We see Japanese running through the flames, their clothes burning; the "Zero" on the track also catches fire and the tents that house the yellows are likewise burning. The gasoline cans begin to explode, one after the other, projecting their flames fantastically.

The confusion is dreadful. But it is nothing compared to what comes a few moments later. There are a series of explosions and, finally, a horrific one that makes the earth tremble.

Ammunition perhaps, an aviation bomb depot, is flying loudly and fragments of everything in the camp are raining down on us.

I imagine that very few have managed to escape from this hecatomb. Now, the most sensible thing to do is get away from here.

I shout some orders and we run as best we can, always north.

When, a couple of hours later, we climb a hill and climb to the top, the great fire is perfectly visible. It is the trees that provide the fuel now. The survivors of our attack will have a lot to do to turn that off, if they ever do.

"Something great," says Texas.

It must be, I guess.

"We will camp here," I say. Two-hour guards. I will do the first.

They all get the best they can. They seek to isolate themselves from the humidity of the soil by forming piles of leaves and branches of the bushes.

We are all dead tired. In a few minutes they sleep heavily while I watch. I think I can have a cigarette now.

I light it, protecting the match with the warrior so that the light does not show. Then I keep the cigarette covered with my hand. The burning tip could be seen from miles away.

With the night there is something cool. I feel a chill and look up at the stars.

I have always thought that the Big Dipper is the most beautiful of the constellations. Now I have two hours to contemplate it uninterruptedly.

* * *

Despite everything, I have slept soundly. I guess I was too tired. But the noise of an engine wakes me up and I see that my colleagues have also been awake.

The plane passes very low, almost skimming the treetops. We are well covered by lush vegetation.

I imagine what happens; the small airfield that we burned down last night has made the Japanese nervous. They must assume that there is a significant allied force around these outlines and seek to discover it.

It is a combat apparatus, a "Zero," which has made the first pass.

Then comes a reconnaissance plane, with fixed landing gear, which flies much more slowly, although low like the other one.

Texas faces his submachine gun and, before I can stop him, fires furiously at the enemy machine. It is very difficult to shoot down an aircraft with small caliber bullets, but it flies very low and any aircraft is vulnerable enough if it is hit at a vital point.

The Japanese apparatus rises sharply. I hope you did not notice the attack you have been subjected to, in this dim light of dawn.

But I can't help but gasp. The device is leaving a trail of black smoke! I watch its rising curve with interest, until the orange flare appears. It has caught fire.

Something detaches from the apparatus, moving away from it; then the huge umbrella of a parachute.

The two gurkhas start running. I imagine that they are going to give a very warm welcome to the Japanese, but I stop worrying about this when I realize that we have "Zero" on us again.

I don't know if he discovered us, but he makes a pass firing his machine guns. And the projectiles are not misdirected, either. We hit the ground and I start to curse the Texas idea. But in our short existence as guerrillas we have already destroyed two enemy planes and dispatched a good number of Japanese. Not bad for newbies.

The "Zero" continues to machine-gun those contours furiously, but they are blind sticks, since afterwards the volleys will stop far from us. This lasts a good quarter of an hour, until he runs out of ammunition.

"It's going to be hot in here in no time," smiles Texas.

Is right. The report that a landing field has been destroyed and an aircraft shot down will make the region popular, no doubt.

"We will leave in a hurry," I order. Be on the lookout for another air strike.

We continue the march and, a little further on, half an hour later, the two Gurkhas join us. They say nothing, but I know that somewhere nearby there is now a Japanese corpse, irreparably pierced by the curved knives of those jungle soldiers.

* * *

We discovered the Burmese village in a small valley not far from the Northern Highway, which winds a few miles beyond. With the Sikh lieutenant's binoculars, which I have appropriated as the chief, I scan the buildings, mostly bamboo, trying to find out if there are Japanese there.

I see people in the colorful clothes that are used in the country, cows wandering peacefully and workers in the next sugar cane fields and rice fields; no sign of Japanese. However, do not trust.

We have been walking through the jungle for five days and our supplies are running out. We barely have some dried bread, cheese and a few cans of preserves.

I pass the binoculars to Texas.

"There are a lot of cattle here," he says. And we have money.

It's true. We carry Chinese dollars and Anglo-Indian pounds. I suppose it will be possible to buy meat in the village. And, of course, any kind of food that they want to sell us.

We all gathered under one of the big trees and discussed the situation.

"We can not appear in the town the whole group" I expose. If there are Japanese and it is a trap, those who do not go will be saved. On the other hand, even if there are no Japanese now, it is logical to think that they will show up sooner or later. Then, the natives will only be able to report what they see; of two men only. Little Gurkha and I will go. The others will wait here, guarding the town. If there are enemies, or if they appear while we are there, the group must flee, heading north. Don't wait. We will try to follow them. If we do not return, and while my absence lasts, the lieutenant will take command ...

I look at Texas stupidly. I haven't bothered to find out his name yet. He smiles.

"Egan" informs ". Lieutenant James Egan.

"Lieutenant Egan" continued. " In turn, he will be replaced if necessary by Lieutenant ...

The Sikh smiled too.

Sing Muzumdar.

"Well, that's it," he finished.

The Gurkha sergeant and I set off, walking slowly down the slope toward the village. In view of how events are unfolding, I cannot help but feel optimistic. Burma is very large and, on the other hand, the terrain is so intricate and the forests so thick, that the Japanese would have to have a man behind each tree to control the territory properly.

In other words: I think we will make it.

We reached the end of the forest, at the edge of the farmland. We crouched there and watched the natives. There does not seem to be any danger; They are busy with their tasks and there is no sign of Japanese soldiers.

I look at Little Gurkha. He looks back at me calmly. The decision is mine.

I make sure the submachine gun is ready and go out into the clearing, leaving the forest. The gurkha follows me, glancing around us.

Nothing happens for a few moments. We continue walking towards the first houses of the town, as if we were in our own territory.

Then someone discovers us and yells something. There is a formidable hubbub in less than it takes to report it. Men, women and children rush to meet us and surround us; but unfortunately I cannot understand what they say.

I turn to Little Gurkha to see if he can interpret for me, but I can't quite ask the question. Shake your head negatively. He also doesn't speak Burmese, or whatever this language is. I know that there are several races and languages in the country.

I just smile left and right and I realize, with a certain start, that we are not going, but that they are taking us. In other words, they are pushing us towards a certain part of the town. I don't know whether to oppose or go along with these people.

I opt for the former. We arrive in front of a bamboo house, more spacious than the others, and the group of Burmese leading us stops.

The wait is not very long, however. A few minutes later an oriental appears at the door and looks at us attentively. Although his face resembles that of other inhabitants of the town, he is dressed in a white western suit.

"English? "asks me.

"American. I am an aviator and I was shot down five days ago "I answer him.

He nods his head. He leans to one side and points us inside. He is inviting us in.

When we do, we find ourselves in a square room, with bamboo mats on the floor. However, it is fresh, and clean, very civilized compared to the life we have led lately.

Our guest claps his hands, and immediately a really attractive Burmese girl brings us cups of tea on a wooden tray.

The conversation does not begin until after having taken a few sips, I suppose this will be the custom of the country.

"I am Dr. Indaw" he tells us. " The village chief is absent but I have a lot of influence here.

"Are there Brits around? "I ask.

Shake your head negatively.

"The allied forces withdrew to the North," he informs us. " Also to the West, on the way to Yunnan, in China. We know that small guerrillas operate around here, remnants of units destroyed by the invaders, but we have hardly seen one or the other. The Japanese occupy the country and come here from time to time. My advice, if it is of any use to you, is to try to get to Manipur.

Manipur is northwest of this point. It's what we planned to do anyway.

"Can they sell us food? "Is my next question.

"We are scarce," he says. The Japanese take everything they find, but I think we can give them some rice.

"Perhaps" I observe "it is possible for us to acquire a cow.

Now Dr. Indaw smiles kindly:

"I'm afraid not," he explains. " The villagers are Buddhists and cannot kill animals. Nor will they sell any of their cows to be slaughtered. They will have to settle for rice. His companions will understand, surely.

You have guessed that there are not just two of us. Anyway, this does not matter. These Burmese seem friendly and undoubtedly fear the Japanese enough to hate them.

We will take what they give us and go on our way. We will stumble upon more towns and I hope they are all like this one.

We do not have the opportunity to continue exchanging impressions. In the vicinity of the village, a hand grenade explodes and shots are heard. I think I recognize the fire of our weapons, although I can be wrong.

What could have happened? I run to the door of the house and put the binoculars towards the slope where our companions stayed.

I can't see anything and, on the other hand, the fire has stopped. Those noises may have come from somewhere else. I am about to leave the village in a hurry, as soon as they give us the promised food.

However, it is not only we who are concerned; the natives seem very excited. A man comes running and talks to our guest. I see your face darken.

"Japanese! "tells me". A truck loaded with them comes along the way.

I can already hear the noise of the engine. Too late to win the forest without being seen.

Then the doctor shouts orders. Then it comes back to us.

"My people will hide them. Go quick! "tells us.

He leaves, no doubt to meet the dangerous visitors, while Little and I, led by a Burmese, are led past one of the buildings in the village. The guide signals us to climb the ladder that is leaning against the wall of bamboos.

We do it quickly and find ourselves in a kind of hayloft, partly filled with dry grass.

Since this is higher than the rest of the buildings, we can see very well what happens below. Along the way a light truck appears, with the hated red discs on the sides. Some eight or ten soldiers are crowded inside.

And something else. I can see light-colored hair and my heart skips a beat. There is a woman with them, a white woman.

Then when she turns her head, I recognize her. It's Doris McDonald!

What happened to the others? It is not difficult to imagine. Somehow, those yellow monkeys have surprised the party, killing them all. Less her. They must have other plans. When I think of them, I feel a highly unpleasant discomfort in the pit of my stomach.

They go down to earth. They are sent by a young, tiny officer with his samurai sword at his side and a high-pitched voice, barking orders in their damned language.

"Dr. Indaw meets them and the officer talks to him. I see him pointing to one of the houses and I guess he is providing lodging. But the officer does not enter there. It is Doris who is pushed by one of the soldiers, who remains at the door, on guard.

The officer leaves with the doctor and the other soldiers remain next to the truck.

I look at Little Gurkha.

"If we climb on the roof," I say, "we can get close enough to throw grenades at the soldiers next to the truck. Hopefully we will destroy them all. So we'll only have two men left to deal with.

The little gurkha nods his head.

"Yes, sir," he says laconically.

I think I have read something about some bomb rosaries used by the Philippine guerrillas. It involves stringing a few grenades through the rings, pulling the safety of one of them and throwing them. They must all explode with that effect called "sympathy."

We have a few with us. I prepare five, fastening them with my belt. The shorts I am wearing are a little tight on me and I won't need them.

So we slipped out of the hayloft onto the roof. This is too flexible. I know it is strong and will hold our weight perfectly, but it sways under our feet in a somewhat reassuring way.

We went to the roof of the next house and then to another. We are already in front of the truck.

I peek a bit. The soldiers are sitting on the ground, smoking and talking loudly. It's the moment; it must be done before they disperse.

I unsnap one of the grenades and reach out. Here they go!

He threw them with good aim and I see that they describe an arc, going to fall in the middle of the group, right on the head of one of the soldiers.

He screams frantically.

I hide and the explosion sounds. Not all are dead, but none have risen. Little Gurkha throws another grenade and the screaming stops.

I run to the other end of the roof. From there I can see the soldier who is guarding the place where Doris has been locked up.

Indeed, it comes running, glued to the opposite wall. I shoot him a short burst with the submachine gun, and the ground jumps past his feet.

He drops one knee to the ground and turns, discovering me. He raises his rifle, too late, however. The next download ends with him.

"Doris! "scream". Get down on the ground and don't move!

Now the Japanese officer is alone. I understand that we have to finish him off quickly and get out of here. This truck won't be the only one doing patrols around here. We are in danger of another showing up.

From the roof we enjoy a good position. Little Gurkha on one side and I on the other; the Japanese will not know where to look for us. Most likely, he will go to the place where he left his men with the truck.

It is precisely what happens. With the trunk leaning forward, holding the sword in the left hand and brandishing a pistol in the right, the officer runs towards the truck.

I unsecured another grenade. I slowly count to three and throw it about a yard ahead of him.

It bursts loudly. The officer has fallen. One leg is almost detached above the knee; he is face down, leaning on his hands and screaming like a wild beast.

Little Gurkha has already come down from the roof. He runs like an arrow towards the Japanese, with his wavy knife in hand. You don't have a second of hesitation. He grabs him by the neck and stabs him with the knife, once, twice, three times, until he collapses and stops screaming.

I drop to the ground from the roof. It's barely seven or eight feet tall.

"Doris! "scream". Doris!

The girl appears around the corner. He walks as if his legs have become rubber, as they bend with every step. He comes up next to me and I smile at him.

"It's all over," I tell him, smiling. " We can...

But she doesn't listen to me. She is clinging to my arm, her head resting on my shoulder. His back shakes, but I don't hear a sound.

"Okay, calm down," I say. The danger has passed. Let's get out of here right now.

The crisis passes quickly. Take a step back and smile bravely.

Some natives and Dr. Indaw arrive. He looks sadly at the corpse of the Japanese officer.

"There will be retaliation," he says slowly.

I understand your point of view. We have to do something.

"Is there a river running around here? I ask him.

"El Mu. Less than two miles.

As I think I remember, the Mu is a tributary of the Irrawaddy. It is between the latter and the Chindwin.

"Order the bodies to be loaded into the truck," I tell him. Let them put their weapons there too. And, prepare the rice that they are going to give us.

Everything is done quickly. They load the bodies of the Japanese in the truck and give us a couple of sacks of wheat of about ten pounds each. Then the doctor does not want to accept any payment for him.

I examine the truck. His body is very battered; A rear wheel has blown out, but we're only going to cover a short distance. We can do it. The doctor comes with us, to show us the way.

Doris, the doctor and I went up to the cabin. Little Gurkha climbs, to the rear. I start the engine. It works perfectly. Slowly, because of the damaged wheel, we made our way down the muddy road.

It took us half an hour to do the two miles, but we got there. The doctor points with his hand.

"There you have it," he says.

The river runs its course in a box along a valley. The path narrows, but I manage to descend close to the shore.

I brake and we left the vehicle. I tell the gurkha to collect all the hand grenades the Japanese are carrying, and when we get them off the truck and put the rice aside, I climb back into the cab and release the brakes.

The truck slides into the river, picking up speed. The road bends north, to take a course parallel to the current, but I do not take the curve. I jump to the ground and manage not to lose my balance. I see how the truck hurtles towards the river, disappearing under its yellowish waters.

I go back to the others. I shake the doctor's hand.

"Thanks for everything," I say briefly.

"Good luck," he answers.

IV

Little Gurkha offers me a, cigarette. We have stopped in the middle of that endless jungle. By my reckoning we have not advanced to the border for more than fifty or sixty miles, which is discouraging.

I notice that the cigarette pack is almost empty. I look in my pockets and find that we only have one more, which is in the middle. The alternative is this: either we quit smoking or we take cigarettes from the Japanese.

We have also finished with the provisions that we got off the plane and, from this moment, we will have to start with the rice and with anything that we can provide ourselves by our own means.

I have not asked Doris about the ambush in which our companions perished. They are already dead and there is no use knowing more details.

We have a problem. We lack kitchenware. We need something to cook the rice in. Little Gurkha solves the situation by cutting off the top of one of the canteens. I think that cooked rice, without even salt, is going to be horrible. I would like to be able to add something tastier, meat, for example.

I suppose this jungle will be full of animals, but we only see two species in abundance: birds with the appearance of cockatoos, and monkeys.

"How are you? I ask Doris.

"Well. Give me a cigarette, will you? "answers.

I give one to her and she lights it up with mine. The matches that we have left will not last forever either.

"We could shoot down one of those birds," I tell Little Gurkha.

Shake your head negatively.

"They are very hard" he informs me ". They have bad taste. Better, we'll hunt a monkey.

Doris shudders.

"What a horrible thing! He comments.

"It's meat" I smile. " It may make cooked rice seem more palatable to us.

Little Gurkha nods. Although he provided himself with a submachine gun when we collected the equipment from the plane, he did not detach his rifle with a telescopic sight. I guess he must be a top marksman.

I see him face the gun and take careful aim. There is a flock of monkeys in one of the nearby trees. Gently squeeze the trigger and the apes scream hideously as soon as the detonation sounds. Then, after tripping over some branches, a monkey falls to the ground. He is still alive. The gurkha runs towards the animal and finishes it off with his long knife.

He then ties it to a low branch and begins to peel off the skin. It's a disgusting scene. The resemblance of anthropomorphs to man is too disturbing and I am beginning to have my doubts about whether it improves rice.

Once skinned, the bug causes me terrible nausea. It looks like the corpse of a child. Doris has turned her head in another direction. I understand that it will not be possible for us to devour that.

And I tell the gurkha.

"The monkey is good" tries to convince us.

"Not to mention it" I smile. We will eat rice alone. The meat for you.

You don't understand it, but we do what I propose. We light a small fire and cook a portion of rice in the makeshift kettle. Then the gurkha prepares another for him, with the cursed monkey meat.

The rice is really bad; a gelatinous mass, with a smoky taste. The worst thing is the lack of salt. I remember reading that ancient American prairie hunters seasoned their food with gunpowder for want of the necessary seasoning.

I extract a round from one of the magazines I carry and remove the shell. I taste the gunpowder, but can't find a taste similar to salt. Rather like minced charcoal, so I spit it out quickly and finish my rice.

Not only is the food disastrous, but lacking cutlery, we have to use our fingers. I look at Doris and I can't help laughing. Her eyes widen, apparently very surprised; then, as if realizing how humorous the situation is, he laughs.

I haven't shaved in nine days. We are not even half clean either; I, at the very least, must look bizarre. For a few moments we laughed like crazy. I know that, in this moment, we have broken the tension that dominated us all these days.

"I'm sure we'll get out of this alive" I tell Doris. If we still want to laugh, we can cope with whatever comes next.

The gurkha looks at us, continuing to eat his monkey rice. He doesn't laugh. You are sure to be thinking how strange white people are, and you may be right.

"We are the happiest people in the world to laugh in a situation like this" smiles Doris. And, also, the dirtiest.

"I listened! The gurkha raises a hand.

My heart skips a beat. Japanese?

I only hear a kind of muffled grunt. They come from our right.

I look questioningly at the gurkha.

"The boar! He whispers in a very low voice.

Edible meat! The thought electrifies me. I pick up the submachine gun and point into the woods.

"We will catch him! "I order." Stay here, Doris!

The gurkha takes his rifle and we slide as quietly as possible towards the place where the noises are coming from. My partner knows how to walk this terrain much better than I do. Take the lead and I curse the dead branches and the litter on the ground.

I finally catch up. He has dropped to the ground and is pointing forward. I kneel down and peek through the undergrowth. In a small clearing, about fifty yards ahead, there are two hairy beasts, similar to the common pig. Two wild boars whose mere contemplation makes my mouth fill with water.

I shoulder the submachine gun and take aim.

The gurkha brings his mouth to my ear.

"To the little one" indicates in a very low voice.

It seems silly to me. It's going to cost us the same, so I aim for the biggest one and pull the trigger.

I am lucky to knock the animal down; but the other does not run away. He starts puffing and charges towards us at full speed.

The gurkha yells something; I don't understand what he means, but I take aim again and shoot the little boar. The discharge stops abruptly; no matter how hard I pull the trigger, I can't get it to work. The gurkha runs to the left. I've gotten in front of him and he needs space and visibility to shoot.

I pull the lever to eject the jammed cartridge without success.

The wild boar comes running like a locomotive, its fangs covered in foam. With them he can give me a dislike, crippling me badly.

I drop the machine gun and unsheathe the Japanese bayonet that I appropriated a few days ago, but I don't think I will be able to use it effectively.

Then a shot sounds. Only one, but the boar collapses, kicking furiously with its front legs, still trying to get close to me.

The bullet broke his spine. Little Gurkha has an exceptional eye; It has saved me from an extremely dangerous situation.

I approach the wounded boar, deliver the coup de grace, plunging the bayonet into its neck. A jet of blood jumps out and everything ends quickly.

The Japanese who owned this blade previously took care to keep it sharp.

The gurkha meets me. He carries the rifle under his arm and something that looks like a smile is drawn on his lips. With these Asians it is difficult to know which card to stick with.

"The female attacks whenever the male kills himself," he tells me. Instead, the male flees and abandons the female.

Now I understand his determination to shoot the smallest of the wild boars, that is, the female. The balance of my mistake consists of the seconds of tension that I have suffered and two dead animals, when we would have had enough with one.

"We will cut the hams," I suggest. " We will eat like kings.

The gurkha knows how to do it. We then carry the four legs of our prey and return to Doris. I do not tell you about my adventure, since I have played a not very graceful role in it.

The campfire is rekindled and we place one of the boar's legs over the flames, skewering it on a stake that Little Gurkha cuts.

When it finishes roasting, it is partly burned and partly, almost raw; but it is the most delicious thing I have eaten since leaving the Assam base.

Doris also lives up to the meat, and the little gurkha, despite the amount of rice and monkey he has eaten, eats a good portion. We all feel better.

It is not, however, what I know, says a quiet meal. Strange noises come from the forest. There is howling, something that looks like barking and, to top it all off, a series of shrieks and something that sounds like crazy laughter.

Doris looks at me apprehensively. I turn to the gurkha.

"The jackal and the hyena" explains this, very calm. Wild dogs.

We lit a cigarette from our meager supply and I begin to disassemble the submachine gun to unlock it. I get it easily and I'm putting it back together when a kind of dry cough comes to us, on the wings of the wind, followed by a deep, hollow roar that makes the earth tremble.

The gurkha does not wait for us to ask him.

"The tiger" he says briefly.

We are in the domain of wild animals, less fearsome, however, than the children of the rising sun who occupy this once peaceful land.

The wild animals will feast on the remains of the wild boars, but following a preferred turn, according to categories. In this, men still have much to learn from the beasts.

I have finished my homework.

"A little nap is necessary" I smile. We are going to have a laborious digestion and there is no supply of bicarbonate.

We lay down to sleep in the shade of the tropical forest. The rains have already stopped and the land is dry.

* * *

The Chindwin runs at our feet. There are no roads in this part of the country.

That there are no roads means that the Japanese cannot use motorized troops profusely in these territories. Thus, we are more sure of not having unpleasant encounters.

However, you don't have to look far to find these persistent little yellows. They have organized a patrol system using navy barges. We observe how one of them anchors near the shore and disembarks a platoon of twelve soldiers: They wade through the stream with the water at the waist, keeping their weapons high and disappear into the jungle.

Two sailors remain on board. I suppose there must be more of the crew; at least three and one officer.

The wisest thing to do would be to get away from there, but yesterday we smoked our last cigarette and our supplies have run out. There is no doubt that the boat will be provided with the things that we need; therefore, we will risk paying them a visit.

We sit on the ground, at a point from which we can comfortably watch the boat. As we eat the last bit of roast boar we have left, the crew jumps ashore. The sun is really hot and the metal boat will be a furnace at this hour.

There are, as I suspected, three sailors and an officer. They light a bonfire under a tree near the shore and prepare their food. It is an ideal occasion to crawl close to them and dispatch them with a couple of grenades.

But the patrol that has landed cannot be far behind. If they hear the detonations they can undertake the return to pace of charge and it would be a bad business. The system we use must be different.

"We will wait until it gets dark" I say then. " There will be a man on duty on deck, at least. And it will watch the shore preferably. The sergeant and I will swim and climb aboard the other side.

Doris looks at me wearily. The journey is being very hard. It is not physical exhaustion, however, that depresses her the most. It is the uncertainty, the nervous tension of this march through enemy territory where every moment can be the last.

What is my part in the plan? "question.

"Expect. Wait here. For the work that we are going to do, we are enough. If it goes wrong, continue the path north, following the river. Just eighty miles north is Sittaung. The city will have fallen into the hands of the Japanese, but to the west of Sittaung, less than twenty miles away, runs the border of Manipur, friendly territory. That will be her goal if she is alone, and ours if we continue together. I would say "I add smiling", that we will succeed and we will get out of Burma without receiving a simple scratch.

Paro, despite my light tone, there are black omens floating in the air. The gurkha has nothing to say. And Doris goes through a crisis of exhaustion and despair. However, this attack on the barge has to be carried out.

Without food we are lost. We have to try.

The shadows lengthen as the sun walks towards sunset. Soon we will have to embark on the adventure of defeating and annihilating four Japanese, silently.

There is the possibility that the disembarked patrol will come back on board as night falls, but I think it will most likely take a whole day or more to return. Anyway, we will take the risk.

When it is getting dark I feel something like a nervous breakdown. It is a concern that I try to hide. I know that my colleagues trust me and I must not betray them.

If we even had a few cigarettes, I think this wait would be easier for me. Doris, suddenly, seems to have guessed my thought.

He looks in his small bag for a cloth designed to contain a Japanese Army gas mask, which we caught from one of the corpses that we threw into the river a few days ago.

He takes something out of it and hands it to me. I make a surprised gesture. It is a crumpled pack of Japanese cigarettes, badly damaged. It has quite a few.

"I was saving it for an extraordinary occasion," he says slowly.

"This" is an extraordinary occasion. She is going to be left alone, here in the middle of the Burmese jungle, while we go out to undertake an action from which we may not return.

We light our cigarettes and smoke for a few minutes. From time to time I scan the site where the Japanese are. They may not go back on board and sleep ashore, although this is unlikely.

Indeed, as soon as it gets darker they leave the shore and get on the boat. They lower the flag of the rising sun. A sailor stands guard on deck, armed with a rifle and a fixed bayonet. The others disappear through the hatches. When they turn on the lights, they close these hatches, although, not quite, because of the heat, so that some rays are filtered out.

I think it's dark enough for our purposes.

"Let's go? I say to the gurkha.

He stands up and puts his rifle aside. We will carry only the pistols and bladed weapons.

"Anytime, captain," he answers.

I turn to Doris.

"It won't take long," I tell him. We will be back.

She does not answer. We slide silently down the slope, until we reach the bank of the river, above the place where the boat is anchored. Thus, when we have to swim, we will do it with the current. I don't want to think about the bad time Doris is going to have, waiting for our return.

We moved through the bushes on the shore, through the growing darkness. It's going to be a moonless night, very fitting for the company.

Something is haunting my brain as we travel these last few yards in order to reach a favorable place to jump into the water. It bothers me extraordinarily not to find it. There is a detail that I have not taken into account when planning the matter, but I do not fall into what it may be.

I think about it for these short minutes without actually solving the problem.

Finally, we stop. From here we can swim comfortably, the boat is enough downstream. I wrap my pistol in a plastic bag of the kind that contained dried bread and give another to the gurkha to do the same operation with his revolver.

I hope they will be effective in preventing the guns from getting wet. Then we wade into the muddy stream until the water is above our waist. Then we began to swim, slowly so as not to raise foam or make the slightest noise.

The thought that I have forgotten something, something important, tortures my mind, but there is nothing I can do to resolve this situation.

V

The water is warm. This bath would be a pleasure in other circumstances. Anyway, what worries me the most is that feeling of unease at having forgotten something.

However, I have moved on. This you should remember refers to a conversation at the base in Assam. Yes, that was, something a colleague told me about the Chindwin. What was it?

Suddenly, I start to feel cold. What they told me referred to the Chindwin, of course, "Be careful not to fall into the waters of the Chindwin," was what they told me, "it's a swarm of crocodiles."

Crocodiles!

It is too late for regrets. We only have to swim a couple hundred yards, more than enough for us to figure out whether or not it's true about the crocodiles. I wonder if the gurkha knows this.

Most likely you know. Only, being a good soldier, if a superior, me, says to swim in the Chindwin, Little gurkha has nothing to say. I have affection and admiration for this individual of another race who fights valiantly by our side.

Every moment I wait for the deadly jaws of a crocodile to close on my body. This sensation is very acute, especially in the feet, which seem to touch foreign objects with every movement I make.

However, we reached the side of the boat without incident. The worst comes when I grabbed the low gunwale and made me on deck. At this last moment I almost feel like screaming. But everything ends well; I am already on board, hunched over, bayonet in hand, waiting for my companion, less than four yards from the sentry, who is quietly smoking a cigarette.

I can see her blurred figure with each suck she takes. The gurkha meets me silently. I consider the situation for a moment.

The sentry remains motionless, smoking. Between him and us is the mouth of a hatch, about a yard and a half high. Only his head is visible from here, since he no longer paces up and down.

I signal the gurkha to go around ahead, I will go behind. We have to silently eliminate him if we are to be successful.

The gurkha nods. He removes the plastic bag from his revolver and I discover my pistol. It will be a last resort to use firearms, but we will do so if necessary.

Then I grasp the bayonet and slide behind the hatch.

I have the sentry less than a step away. If he turned around right now, he probably wouldn't see me. The darkness is deep; he, on the other hand, is at a disadvantage, with that cigarette in his mouth, indicating his position.

You have to act quickly. I sit up and attack. I put my left arm around his neck, so that I press him on the nut so that he cannot utter the slightest cry. At the same time, I bayonet him in the side until the guards.

It squirms so violently that I think it will get out of hand. But the gurkha is already there, wielding the knife like an expert that he is.

I hear the eerie sound of meat and cartilage being ripped apart by my partner's fearsome blade, which nails and cuts like a beast.

The sentry is already an inert weight on my arm. The gurkha puts the sentry's rifle aside and, between the two of us, we grab him by the feet and put him upside down in the water. We carefully release and the Japanese's body silently sinks.

Now that we own the deck, we must wait for someone to come to relieve the sentry. We cannot risk going down the hatch and engaging three men in a place we do not know, but will be very familiar to them.

The minutes pass slowly, but the occasion arrives sooner than we imagined. Someone comes out the hatch and says something. Since I don't understand Japanese, I suppose this sailor will want to speak to the sentry. It is a difficult moment, because nobody is going to answer him.

But the sailor does not suspect what is happening. You must imagine that your partner will be distracted; He comes out on deck and takes a few steps in my direction, getting dangerously close. I'm crouched behind one of the vents, wondering when the time is right to jump on it.

I can barely make out him in the dark, but his white uniform stands out enough that I don't lose sight of him.

Suddenly, the Japanese seems to start a devilish dance. He kicks furiously even though he doesn't make the slightest sound. I jump on him and I understand what happens in a second. The gurkha, using his belt, is trying to strangle him.

I have to help him and that's what I do. I nail my bayonet swiftly, dealing blow after blow. Something hot and slimy is slipping off the grip, sticking to my hand, but I keep nailing and nailing until the sailor is motionless, inert as a sack filled with something soft and heavy.

We make him follow the same path as his companion and I tap the gurkha on the back. This task is going very well for us. I have no doubt that we will succeed and I am in a very good mood.

I motion for Little Gurkha to stand by the hatch and wait.

I'll watch the other one aft, and that's where I slide. Wet clothes make me shiver, but a soldier cannot ask for comforts. I can't help but smile as I consider what a strange kind of soldier I am, a pilot in command of enemy territory.

It would have saved me a lot of time knowing how I would have to wage war; The government has spent a lot of money on my apprenticeship to get, in exchange, a foot combatant of the rarest in the world.

A metallic resonance startles me. The glass window aft, less than two yards from me, has just been opened. The head and shoulders of the third sailor appear through the opening, disappearing almost immediately.

I approach carefully and take a look. That is a small space where the motor of the boat is housed. The sailor must be the mechanic and is reviewing something by the light of a flashlight. He has some tools next to him and he hums an oriental melody of three or four notes.

It will be useless to threaten you with my gun. Even if his life is at stake, he will scream like a damned man. I have him less than a yard away and I don't know how to reduce him to impotence without breaking the silence.

He's working crouched over the engine. Sooner or later you will sit up to stretch your back a little. Then it will be time to disable him, but how?

One hit will be the right thing to do. I holster my bayonet and grip the heavy .45 automatic. With that blue-steel barrel you could put a rhino to sleep. I don't think the yellow's skull is half as strong as that of one of those beasts.

The occasion arrives. The Japanese, still humming the exotic tune, straightens up and pokes his head through the hatch. Unfortunately, he is not turning his back on me, but is looking at me. However, when going from light to darkness, it will take your pupils some time to adjust to it, time which, on the other hand, I do not allow you.

I drop the gun on his head. I have put all the energy of which I am capable after the blow. There is a horrible click and I watch him fall onto the engine, where he freezes. I've crushed the top of his shaved skull. A good hit.

I return to the gurkha. We only have one enemy left on board. We have to think of something to get him out on deck. But, if it takes a long time, you have to look for it.

Little Gurkha points to a point on the shore. I look in that direction and see some small lights emerge. Then a few points of fire glow in the dark, gaining and losing intensity from time to time.

The Japanese patrol! Contrary to what I believed, they return to spend the night on the boat. And we have not finished our work, far from it.

You have to think something quickly. For example, we can gain the shore and lose ourselves in the forest. But in that case, our situation will remain bad. We have no food ... no cigarettes.

This decides me.

"The anchor! "I tell the gurkha." You have to hoist it.

We run to the bow and pull the chain, trying not to make noise.

The bottom is muddy and we managed it without difficulty. Then the boat begins to drift, driven by the current. When the Japanese reach the place where they left it, they will not find it there and will have to think of a way to find out what happened.

We slide, driven by the current, downstream; fortunately we drifted close to shore.

What is the Japanese officer doing? Perhaps it is sleeping, in which case it will be necessary to try to hunt it without loss of time.

The boat suffers a violent collision and begins to turn slowly; we have touched a sandbar, but we are immediately free of it without running aground.

Then there are shouts in Japanese. The officer has realized that we are adrift and is coming to see what happens!

It rises through the hatch opening with such rapidity that it catches us off guard. I react to the moment and pull the butt of my automatic. I knock him over with a single shot and he falls overboard into the water.

"Come downstairs, hurry! I yell at the gurkha.

We rushed through the hatch and searched the two small cabins and the galley. We found weapons, ammunition, groceries and, thank goodness! cigarettes in large quantities. We look for some sea bags and fill them with those treasures.

With regard to weapons I only select a small and deadly submachine gun and ammunition for it. Of the rest, we load generously.

The boat hits a sandbar or mud again and makes me fall flat on my face. But it has remained immobile, which is convenient for us.

We went out on deck with two of those sacks full to our mouths.

Little Gurkha jumps into the river first. The water is up to his neck, but, with his weapons and a sack on his head, he begins to wade without incident. I follow him, equally loaded, and we win the shore.

I think that Doris must have heard the Japanese patrol arrive and is suffering horribly not knowing what has become of us. We went into the forest and walked quickly, following a path parallel to the river. So we have to necessarily go through the place where we left it.

The night is so dark that we can barely make out the trunk of a tree three steps away; we collide with bushes, some thorny, and cast a few curses from time to time.

The gurkha stops abruptly and collides with him.

"I listened! He tells me in a whisper.

There is a rumor of voices, Japanese of course, that sound to our left. The patrol is looking for the barge. They don't seem very excited. Perhaps they think they have lost their way, missing the precise anchor site.

With the darkness that reigns tonight, it is very possible that they will follow the shore and will not discover the stranded boat.

Anyway, we walk in the opposite direction and they cannot, for the moment, suspect our existence.

We resume the march. We no longer feel cool, our clothes are almost dry, and exercise makes me sweat profusely.

It is impossible to calculate the distance traveled by the boat until it ran aground. It shouldn't be much since the Japanese patrol caught up with us easily, walking along the shore.

I reckon we must be getting to the point where we left Doris.

We explore the terrain and find the exact spot. The weapons and bags are there, under a tree, but there is no trace of Doris.

Before I can think for a bit, there is a nearby noise, which makes me shudder. I see a couple of points of fire at close range and I understand that we have a tiger in front of us.

The gurkha drops the load and takes his rifle, ready to fire; such a thing does not suit us. A detonation could send the Japanese hurtling in this direction and we are exhausted. I hold him by the arm.

"Do not shoot! "I warn you". Perhaps he will leave without attacking us.

For a few tense moments, the fiery eyes of the beast remain fixed on us. I wield the Japanese submachine gun. In spite of everything, we will have to shoot if it attacks us.

But that moment does not come. A second later, the phosphorescent eyes stop shining in front of us and we hear the rustle of the bushes in contact with the body of the tiger, which is moving away from us.

What happened to Doris? I remember the presence of the tiger and I feel a chill. Perhaps it has been eaten by one of these beasts, for which a person is nothing but food.

"Doris! I call in a low voice. Then I shout ": Doris!

An extraordinary rumor hangs in the air above my head, overwhelming me. It is something like the noise of dice being shaken inside the cup.

A dark shadow slides down the trunk. I raise the submachine gun and lower it just as quickly.

It's Doris! I have seen her flowing hair. I walk over and see that he is shaking. It was the clash of their teeth that startled me.

He hugs me and keeps shaking.

"Go Go! "I smile, although I too am about to scream." We are here and we bring everything, even cigarettes!

She keeps shaking.

"I thought I was going crazy," she whispers. Those jungle noises, the roars and howls of wild animals. And the eyes! Bright spots that were fixed on me. I had to climb the tree, although I don't know how I managed it.

She is just a girl. And he's not even crying. Just a little scared. That is all. Doris has good wood.

"That's over," I suggest. " We are going to sit down and eat some preserves prepared for the Imperial Army. Then we'll have a cigarette and leave here. Those yellow ones will record all of this as soon as the sun rises.

We open some cans with the help of the bayonet. It occurs to me that there will still be Japanese blood on the weapon, but this is war and you have to go through everything.

The corned beef isn't particularly good at all, but it's better than the rice we've been eating lately, though less than wild boar's feet in my opinion.

Then we light a few cigarettes and rest for a bit. Who Said Japanese Cigarettes Are Bad? A non-tobacco smoker can be given a few and asked later. At least they seem delicious to me.

I look at the luminous dial of my watch. It's half past twelve. You have to get on your way.

We have to put a few miles between this place and us.

"We will go into the jungle," I tell Little Gurkha. As the river follows a North-South course, it will be easy for us to find you again later.

"Yes sir" Little Gurkha rarely has anything to say other than "Yes sir."

Loaded as we go, the going becomes difficult; But I would not leave the contents of these sacks behind for all the gold in the world.

Doris, after the emotions suffered, walks heavily. I put an arm around her waist and try to help her. We moved away from the river by climbing the side of one of these Burmese mountains. The whole country, from what I am seeing, is full of mountains, forming formidable chains that run from North to South, which explains the direction of the rivers.

We continue walking until we pass to the opposite slope. Then I feel as if my legs have turned to rubber. They bend under my weight every moment. Doris is almost exhausted; it would fall to the ground if it weren't for me holding it.

We arrived at a place strewn with rocks. Between them we stumble upon a stream of water, its surface gleaming ghastly in the scant starlight that filters through the trees, which are thinner there.

I decide that it is time to camp.

"Let's stay here," I suggest.

I put Doris on the floor and she stays still. I lift her up a bit and try to remove the stones from under her so she can rest. Then we put down the load and, mortally tired as we are, we lay down to sleep like logs, without even thinking of setting up a guard as prudence would advise.

* * *

The sun is already very high when I wake up. There are parrots, or cockatoos, of brilliant plumage, spying on us from the branches. A family of monkeys squeals and plays around, trying to get a better look at us, but not daring to get too close.

Doris is still sleeping. Not so the gurkha. He is sitting on a high rock and is watching. He is a born soldier. I'm sure he slept much less time than me, preoccupied with the question of surveillance.

I yawn loudly. Doris opens her eyes. We are covered in dust and dirt, with scratched legs and arms and torn clothes; what is said a real calamity.

"But we are alive and we have many things that we needed" I tell Doris, even though she has not asked. How are you this morning?

She smiles.

Better, I think. Yesterday I acted like a fool, but now I'm fine.

"You were wonderful yesterday," I contradict. Like every day. Take a look at the bathroom we have discovered.

There is a fountain here, between the rocks. A few yards below the water pools in a hollow, forming a natural bathtub of clean and crystalline transparency.

"It will be very nice to take a bath" smiles Doris ", but we are missing so many things ...

"One moment! "I warn". We didn't do last night's excursion at all. I'm going to empty the cornucopia and bet she'll be shocked. See.

I empty the sack that I have so laboriously carried. There are ammunition and supplies in it; but I loaded some more things, back in the Japanese boat.

"I am putting things in front of me, on the rock, proudly listing them:

"The officer commanding the boat was a 'dandy.' He had a bottle of cologne, almost full. Toothbrushes not even brand new, still in their case. After-shave cream, which I hope will be to your liking. Nail file and scissors. Shaver with spare blades, although I don't know what I would do with it; Japanese do not usually have beards. It may have been the exception that proves the rule. A mirror; with a silver frame, which I put at your disposal. A red silk kimono that will be small, but that you can wear without any inconvenience. A ring with diamonds, which I am going to put on my little finger to keep as a souvenir, and another with a pearl that will become your property right now. I suppose he would change rings from time to time, since these were in his cabin. We should have examined him before we threw him in the water. Surely he had something else of value with him.

That observation makes Doris lose her smile.

"It was very hard? "question.

"I don't think so" I smile. " We are alive, while those dwarfs are grazing crocodiles at this hour. They had a much worse time; look at this: two combs. In addition, this gold cigarette case that will be for

Little Gurkha "I throw it at him and he catches it in the air", and a lighter, also made of gold, which, likewise, are part of the spoils of war of our brave companion. Toothpaste and a glass eye! I had it in a glass of water. He was one-eyed, the poor thing, that's why he sent a boat on the river instead of being with the imperial navy in a battleship. This eye will serve as my amulet and I will carry it in my pocket as long as I live. What do you think, Doris? I think it was worth it.

Now comes the best. I saved it for last on purpose. A cardboard box containing three beautiful bars of toilet soap.

Doris loses her seriousness again. He laughs cheerfully and unwraps one of the pills, smells it, and shakes his head.

"It will be the most pleasant bath of my life," he says.

"You will be in charge of keeping these treasures in your bag" I order, half jokingly half seriously. If you lose them, I'll arrest you.

Doris searches our bags and pulls out some of the items of clothing that we fortunately took from the plane. Army shorts and shirts, but they are priceless under these circumstances.

"Get out of sight for half an hour," he says, smiling.

"Well" I suppose, "I will send the gurkha to a new lookout post and I will stay by her side to protect her, if necessary.

"No.

"There are beasts" I observe ", and Japanese. I'll tell you what we're going to do. We will both bathe at the same time, so that we can rub each other's backs and we will be clean as a diamond.

"You leave with the gurkha and do not come back here until I have finished my bath," he yells at me with comical anger. I bet the tigers and the Japanese are less dangerous.

I look at Doris thoughtfully. She is, despite her tattered clothes, really attractive.

"I think he's right". We won't be far, however. When done, announce with a voice.

The gurkha and I drift away until the rocks are behind, forming a screen between us and the makeshift bathtub. I light a cigarette and sit on the ground, leaning my back against a tree trunk.

VI

"Captain! Little Gurkha's voice has a strange timbre, unknown to me.

I get up quickly and run over there, preparing the submachine gun in the meantime. There is a small clearing, with rocky ground, probably petrified lava, that runs down the slope into the deep valley.

The gurkha is there, motionless as a statue. There seems to be no danger; So what are you seeing?

I go ahead until I reach him and I see him.

Corpses

Bearded Sikhs, fourteen of them, and three British officers, dead. Shot dead.

Minus one of the British officers. This one, lying a little further, is just a headless log, under which there is a huge pool of dried blood.

The head is about seven or eight steps from the corpse.

Gritting my teeth, I examine the corpse. Features a bullet hole in the shoulder.

The story is easy to piece together. Also, the gurkha is talking about it:

"A guerrilla; like us, the rest of a unit defeated by the Japanese "pauses and lights a cigarette." Defeated, but not defeated. They camped near the water. A Japanese patrol discovered them and waited, in ambush, for them to set off, forming a group. They shot at them from behind the trees; all fell dead, except the young officer, who was wounded. They cut off his head. I've seen how they do it, sir. A Japanese man grabs the condemned man, makes him kneel and pulls his arms, pushing with his knee on the prisoner's back. Then an officer cuts off his head with his sword. Strange people, sir. An army where the officers do the job of executioners.

Strange people, really. I do not intend to condemn the Japanese, or even to prosecute them; I just want to understand them. But this is out of my power at the moment.

I think my joy today has completely vanished. I also believe that it was due to the fact that I forgot, for a moment, that this is war, the most cruel and deadly war in the history of humanity; a war of race and principle like never before.

Those seven steps from the British officer's trunk to his head speak eloquently about this. They beheaded him. Then someone kicked the bloody trophy, adding the last note of what? Cruelty? Indifference?

"We have to bury them," I tell the gurkha.

He nods his head and puts his rifle on the ground.

It would take us hours to dig a grave for so many people. But, in the rocky bed there is a fissure that can help us. We will deposit the corpses there and cover it with stones to prevent beasts from digging up the remains.

It is curious that this has not happened already. The idea occurs to me that the massacre is recent, perhaps it happened yesterday afternoon. It is quite possible that the armies of the massacre are the components of the patrol that disembarked from the barge. If so, they are partially avenged.

We begin the task. During it I seized one of the knives of these brave Sikhs. They are not the same as those of the Gurkhas; they only have a single curve instead of being double. But they seem just as deadly and I prefer it to continue to carry the Japanese bayonet.

The task of placing the corpses in the cavity of the rock is heavy, but covering it with stones is much worse. We work hard, however, and by the time Doris calls us it is finished. I have collected the dog tags of these soldiers to hand over when I return to India. I write a note on a piece of paper, with the numbers of the plates, I put it in one of the canteens that the Sikhs carried and I deposit them in the tomb, covering it with stones as well. Family members may one day want to collect these bodies.

When we return to Doris, she has finished her bath. He has dressed in a new uniform and combs his hair.

"How is the water? I ask, trying to keep sounding optimistic.

I must not have gotten the proper expression, since Doris stares at me and, in turn, answers me with another question:

"What happen?

"Nothing in particular. We found the bodies of British soldiers and buried them.

He shakes his head sadly.

"That will be our end," he says thoughtfully. Die somewhere in this wild country.

"Those yellow monkeys won't get it," I retorted violently. I will wear my brain down to the size of a chickpea, but I will find the solution to our problems and bring them all to India, even if it takes me years to do so. It is a promise. We have been unlucky, losing the other teammates, but the three of us have to live to see the general defeat of the Mikado and his "monkeys".

Suddenly, Doris starts laughing. I don't know whether to make myself uncomfortable or laugh too, but I hear the gurkha give a little laugh.

"Did I say something funny? He asked fiercely.

A good joke "explains Doris", Mikado and monkeys! It matches perfectly.

It was an involuntary pun, but I also find it funny now.

"Okay, we'll take the bath ourselves" I have partially recovered my good humor. Leave the place and be careful not to look in this direction. It could be dangerous for me.

"Is it so irresistible, Captain? Doris smiles.

"You will judge" I reply slightly. In my neighborhood they called me Frankie "the well done."

Doris goes behind the rocks, laughing heartily. It is a magnificent sign. As long as we can laugh, even half, we will have half the battle won.

I undress to dive into the pool; no matter how much of a hurry I am, I cannot do it before the gurkha. He's already in the water when I come in, puffing and flapping like a child.

It seems ridiculous to me; then I consider that I am doing the same, a moment later, and I laugh again. We are in trouble, in the worst of, our life; but there are moments that can be fully enjoyed. To hell with the rest!

I give myself a good dose of soap and, getting out of the water, I rub my body with the greatest enthusiasm. The foam, initially white as snow, turns a grimy chocolate color. You have to get wet again, give yourself a new hand of soap and repeat the operation until the foam does not lose its purity.

Then it's time to take care of the nails. With the scissors I cut out all the ones I have, including the ones for the feet. The gurkha follows the same guidelines as me, except for shaving, since he belongs to one of those fortunate races that have no hair on their faces.

"Would you dare to cut my hair a little, friend? I ask him.

He looks at me very seriously.

"I dare, sir," he says. And, I won't charge you anything for it.

I try to guess if he is joking, but his face, it would be as usual, is devoid of any expression.

Take the scissors and lighten my hair with a few slight cuts. I don't know how the operation is going; but Doris, who has returned to the fountain, seems too smiling.

"Lend me the mirror, please" I ask.

He gives it to me and I have to admit that the gurkha could not make a living in a fancy barber shop. But it has freed me from annoying tresses and, in addition, it has done the work for free.

I can, and plan to, take revenge.

"Now, I'll be a hairdresser" I suppose.

"I don't cut my hair, sir," he replied very seriously.

Perhaps the Gurkhas are one of those races whose religion does not allow anyone to touch their heads or something like that. I decide to leave things as they are and put on my boots. In a clean uniform, freshly bathed and shaved, and even smelling of scented soap, I feel like new.

Now a good feast would be good. Something like lobster with mayonnaise, oysters with champagne, and maybe caviar.

However, it will have to be something else, Canned meat, Japanese; also seasoned with a good appetite, and clear water from the source.

"It is hard to believe that we are in an enemy-occupied country," observes Doris ". Under a bright sun, with this landscape all around, you almost feel at peace with the world.

It is possible that everything looks like this. But not an hour ago we have buried a group of corpses. Do not be fooled. This is a fierce war and we are inside it.

"There is a lot of calm in the environment" I smile.

I hope it last's.

* * *

When we leave the fountain in the middle of the afternoon, I can't help but turn my head and contemplate the place. It has been a pleasant time that we have spent here. The best since all this started. Not all the memories that we will keep from our adventure will be bad.

We headed up the slope opposite the valley where the Chindwin runs. We follow the tracks opened by wild animals, at mid-altitude. It is certain that the boat we attacked last night will not be the only one in the river.

I think we will be safer on this side. We will not march very fast, but we are covering more ground than I originally estimated.

Actually, today it seems that we are in another world different from that of days gone by. There is, floating in the air, an atmosphere of peace, as Doris has already observed.

This is misleading. It can even be dangerous. Living in the Burmese jungle for weeks, slain to our own strength, would be more than hard. Considering the circumstances that the country is occupied for the most part by the Japanese, things are much worse.

The gurkha always walks a little ahead, attentive to our surroundings, stopping from time to time to listen or to look in a certain direction. He is a magnificent guide and a top fighter. He never talks about heat, fatigue or the like. He is ready to do his duty at any time.

I try to imitate him to the best of my ability. There is life behind the tangle of trees that surrounds us. Not many animals are seen, however. They avoid our encounter with ease, since nature endowed them much better than human beings. They smell us and hear us at great distances and withdraw.

That is why it surprises me that a tribe of monkeys rush to meet us, screaming like mad, then discover us and jump, down the slope, from branch to branch, like hairy and tiny Tarzanes.

They've been scared of us, but someone scared them before. The sun is almost touching the top of the mountains that we have to our left, whose peaks protrude above this one through which we walk.

The gurkha makes a hand sign, a stop sign. We stop while he creeps into the jungle. After a few steps we no longer see him. We wait in silence.

He returns after a few minutes, as cautiously as he left.

"Japanese" he says.

One word, but one that brings us back to reality.

"How many? "I ask.

"Eight, with an officer, They are close and coming straight towards this site.

We are not in a good place. The crest of this mountain is bare and there are also clearings below. It is one of those places in the Burmese jungle where large masses of lava prevent the lush vegetation from growing, leaving spaces in clear.

Trying to backtrack, hide to the side of the treeline, or try to silently cross paths with the Japanese column would be desperate. They could discover us and we are only two men and one woman against nine hardened Japanese soldiers, masters of fighting in the jungle.

I look at the rock formations on the right. That is like a natural castle. It can help us, to hide and defend ourselves well, if the case comes, even if the prospects are bad if we have to fight.

The decision is mine; our lives depend on it and this causes me a slight discomfort in the pit of my stomach. Worst of all, I only have a few minutes to make this decision.

I realize that the most disastrous thing will be indecision. I point to the rocky group.

"We'll hide up there," I say.

The gurkha nods his head. Doris not even that.

We walked quickly and climbed towards the ridge. The formation is about twenty feet high, and as we see when we reach the top, there is enough room there to hide comfortably.

The problem is that the Japanese register that. If they pass by, everything will be fine. I hope they do. However, sunset is very near. It is a good place to camp in front of us, clear, in the shape of a half moon. If they don't stop here, the night will fall on them in the middle of the jungle.

This I should have thought before, I reproach myself. Then when I sneak a peek across the rocky group, I see the remains of a bonfire, half-consumed sticks, and a black circle on the ground.

Someone has used this as a camp on occasion. Perhaps these same soldiers who are coming now, in which case we can count on them staying the night. The thought doesn't make me very happy.

I focus my attention on the jungle; I look towards the place where the Japanese should appear, according to the information of the gurkha.

A few more minutes and they appear, indeed.

They must have had a quiet patrol, because they chatted animatedly, walking slowly after their officer.

My fears are confirmed. The officer, smaller and thinner than any of his men, barks orders in a shrill voice, his glasses gleaming as they reflect the last rays of the setting sun.

Two men run to the nearest trees and stockpile firewood, cutting branches with their machetes. With this and a few armfuls of litter they will have enough to spend the night.

The officer keeps barking more orders. Automatically, the soldiers perform another task that intrigues me. They set about digging a small trench about ten or twelve inches wide by the same depth. Then, at a distance, they excavate another, but much longer.

They carry small shovels in their backpacks, as in any army, but their use should be dedicated to obtaining trenches and marksman pits.

On the other hand, those small ditches would not serve as a shelter or a cat, least of all a man. I think about how ideal it would be if those guys put down their weapons and gathered in a group in front of us.

A couple of grenades and submachine guns would account for them in an instant, which would make me feel calmer and safer. These soldiers have been fighting for years in China, Manchuria and elsewhere. Even if they do not discover us, they can find our tracks in the camp of the source and go in pursuit.

Yes, the thought of eliminating the Japanese patrol is pleasant from my point of view. If only a good opportunity presented itself ...

What is this? They are laying down their weapons!

I begin to see clearly. The Japanese, like all living things in creation, are subject to certain physical needs. But in the very disciplined

Japanese Army, even this has been planned. Now I understand what those very small trenches mean.

They have been on their patrol through the jungle all day; this is the moment when they will evacuate the bodily needs that I just mentioned, but they will do it as clean and disciplined people, inside the ditches, which they will fill with earth later.

In a few moments they have lowered their belts, they lowered their pants to their knees and they squatted on the ditches, with their backs to us; the officer on the smallest and his men, perfectly in line, on the largest.

I exchange a glance with the gurkha and see that his eyes shine. Better time than this will never happen.

Quickly, I hold four grenades, passing a rope through the rings. The time to send our greetings will come when the task of evacuating the bowels has begun; so, with my finger inside the ring of one of the bombs, I wait.

When I see that the operation has started, I pull the safety and reach out. I count three seconds; then I drop the four bombs. The line of Japanese is so close that I could have pulled more, without falling short, but I prefer not to force my luck.

We lower our heads to protect ourselves behind our natural parapet and the tremendous explosion sounds.

The gurkha and I peek out again. There are some figures lying down; the others run to where they have left their weapons. But trying to run when, simultaneously, they have to pull up their pants and hold them down so they don't fall off again is superhuman.

The gurkha, with his rifle, and I with the submachine gun, we shot them down as easily as if we were in a shooting gallery. When not a single one is left standing, we exchange a smile. This is something that we should never tell because it is incredible, but it will fill us with satisfaction for the rest of our lives.

Only Doris remains lying at the bottom of the hollow, with her head on her knees and her hands crossed over her neck.

The gurkha and I jumped out of hiding and ran towards the remains of the Japanese patrol. The position of the corpses is not very graceful, really. Most have knee length pants; I think this makes up for the bitter memory left in my mind by the group of Sikhs and British that we buried this morning, especially the one with the beheaded officer as stupidly as cruelly.

"This man is alive! The gurkha yells at me.

I see him lean over the Japanese officer and at the same time draw his fearsome, twisted steel blade.

"Wait! "I order.

I approach him too and verify that he is right. One of those coincidences that are lavished so much in the novels has just happened to the Japanese. He has been knocked out by a bullet that grazed his skull, causing some concussion, but he is unharmed.

The gurkha looks at me questioningly. It is an eloquent look; he continues with the knife in his hand, ready to slaughter the Japanese as soon as I move my finger.

"Bring a couple of belts" and I point towards the corpses "; We will tie his hands behind his back and take him prisoner.

The gurkha seems not to have understood what I am saying. The Japanese is moving and growling something. We are just two men with a vague idea of where we want to go and the path we must follow to achieve it. How are we going to carry a prisoner?

I understand all of this but I can't bring myself to coldly kill this lemon-faced guy who has caused us the trouble of not putting our heads in a better position so that the bullet would go through his yellow brain.

"Do what I say Sergeant" I bark peremptorily.

The gurkha, shaking his head from side to side, obeys. It comes with two leather straps and, between the two of us, we tie the officer's wrists behind his back, finishing pulling up his pants, fastening his belt and leaving everything so that he can walk.

A canteen of the same extinct Japanese helps us to revive him. I pour the water over his head. Since he's on his back now, he coughs violently. I think that part of the water has entered his nose which is the same to me, on the other hand.

Fully recover your faculties and open your eyes. I realize how alert he is when he sees the look of hatred that he directs me. If you could kill yourself with your eyes, I would have fallen to the ground, a corpse, at this moment.

Anyway, I am very confident in thinking that this guy is harmless because he is slightly injured and has his hands tied behind his back.

He proves me otherwise in the next few seconds. He stretches his legs and makes me a kind of lock that knocks me down cleanly. Then before I am out of astonishment, he's grabbing me by the neck, threatening to choke me, and holding his hands! Only with the legs.

I hear a noise like a bass drum. The pressure on my neck loosens. Another one of those hollow noises and I feel free. The Japanese is writhing on the ground when I get up and check the origin of those sounds that have saved me.

The gurkha is giving him a lot of back kicks that make my hair stand on end. I rub my aching neck and cry out:

"Okay now, Sergeant!

Drop the punishment, but pull his knife.

"Did I kill him now, yes? "question.

It would be the most logical thing to do, but I shake my head negatively.

"I do not tell him". Tie her ankles.

I see that Doris has also come down from our rocky castle; it doesn't come close, however. This war thing is terrifying and I understand that it disgusts anyone.

There are things to do, however. My main concern is to preserve life as long as possible, so the rest is secondary. I am dedicated to searching the soldiers' backpacks.

There are cigarettes, and cans of preserves. I also collect hand grenades and everything that I think we can transport and can be useful to us.

Then when we are done with everything, I tell the gurkha to untie the prisoner's feet, put a gag on him, and provide me with a good rope.

Of course there are no strings there. But conscientiously, he has collected the belts of the fallen and with them we serve ourselves to my liking. I have devised to tie a strap to each arm and we will take him in the middle so that, holding the straps, we will have him at an equal distance from one to the other, preventing him from using any of his circus tricks.

We set off when the night is completely closed, but you have to get away from those neighborhoods.

Always heading north, we go into the jungle. We do a new march of two and a half hours.

Then, when it is no longer time to look for a good place to camp, we lie down under a big tree. We tie the Japanese well and we tie the straps that hold the arms to our wrists. If you make any movement during the night we will notice it immediately.

We are so tired that we don't even think about having dinner. Tomorrow will be another day.

Now you have to sleep.

VII

I wake up with a start. My first impulse is to make sure the prisoner is still with us.

With the consequent alarm, I verify that I am alone under the tree, that the Japanese is not attached to the other end of the leash, as it should be.

But a look around me reassures me. I see the gurkha, with his usual fierce grin, rifle in hand; in front of him is our prisoner sitting on the ground.

Doris is a little further, combing her beautiful hair, now that she has the necessary supplies.

It's very early, barely six thirty, according to my watch. As usual, I have slept more and better than everyone else. I suppose these are legitimate command prerogatives.

"Good morning everyone" he smiled. I see that they are still as early risers as ever. I'm going to wash up a bit. Then we'll eat something and get going. How has the Japanese behaved?

Little Gurkha remains motionless.

"I was restless, sir," he replies. But he calms down a lot when a gun is pointed at him.

The toilet I alluded to earlier consists of pouring a little water from the canteen into the hollow of your hand and rubbing your eyes with it. There is no running water here.

It has the advantage that little time is used. When I'm done, Doris is opening some cans. I release our prisoner's hands and hand him one.

We eat with a good appetite. Even the Japanese seem hungry, which is understandable considering that we didn't have dinner the night before.

It is then, when we resume the march, with the prisoner well tied up again and gagged, when I clearly realize the hindrance that results in taking him with us.

Killing him is out of the question. I know perfectly well that any group of commands would have already dispatched it, but I am not a command; just an american rider who am riding a hundred mile ride very much against my will.

As for releasing him, it would be like killing ourselves. The Japanese have to know where to look for their compatriots. So he would organize a hunt that would finish us off quickly.

It's inhuman, monstrous, but I can't stop thinking about how convenient it would have been for us if this guy had died when we attacked his patrol. An inch lower, and the bullet that dislodged him would have pierced his brain.

I get all these thoughts because, to my amazement, I realize that we Caucasians are not clean wheat either, at least not quite.

The forest is now so thick that we cannot walk except by making continual detours, describing eses between tree and tree, so that each mile of the way north has really cost us two or three.

For some strange reason I am remembering one of my youth readings: Kipling's "The Jungle Book." The flora and fauna are certainly very similar to those of India.

"Watch out! "The cry of the gurkha brings me back to reality.

I wield the submachine gun, but the danger that it announces to us could not be conjugated to bullets, if it were unleashed. It is about wasps' nests that are on a thicket, next to the track that we follow. They are round and elongated, like rugby balls.

I have a strange idea. Perhaps these dangerous insects can be of use to us.

"Come here, sergeant," he ordered the gurkha.

He meets me and I point out the hornets' nests.

"We have macutos provided with zip closure" I observe. If we do it cleanly, we can put those hornets' nests in two of them and close quickly, taking the swarms with us.

The face of the gurkha is quite a poem. I don't doubt that he likes me, but I also know that he thinks me a little crazy. However, as usual, he agrees:

"Yes sir.

We put Doris in charge of guarding the prisoner and we get to work. I place the bag under one of the hornets' nests. The gurkha grabs him and thrusts him inside with lightning speed. Then, with a sharp jerk, I close the zipper.

"Excellent! "I comment." Not one escaped.

We proceed to deal with the second with the same dexterity, but with less luck. Three or four wasps jump out of the bag before it is closed and go prodding at will until we slap them to death.

The gurkha has been lucky. Almost all the pecks were carried on the legs. They have given me theirs in legs and arms; but one of them, the damned one, chose my nose as a target. To the touch I feel that it is taking an alarming size.

I must have a horrible face. Doris laughs and even the prisoner looks astonished. Maybe I should ask Doris for the mirror to personally check the chosen one from the sting, but I decide not to. Better leave it. After all, this is temporary.

We resume our march and what I feared arises. The gurkha is too disciplined to ask the question, but Doris asks:

"What do you want those wasps for, Captain?

I touch my nose. It is even more swollen than the last time I recognized it.

"It is difficult to explain" I answer. I have only thought that they can be useful to us on occasion. That is why I have captured them.

"That is to say, you have no idea what you are going to use them for.

"Something like that.

Doris shrugs expressively. I try to imagine what I would have thought if I had seen someone else perform the maneuver; Then I discard the thought because I don't like it.

I notice then that the path we are following does not make me see the sun walking from our right to our left, which makes us suspect that we are not exactly following the northern route. You have to orient yourself again.

Getting away from the Chindwin would be a catastrophe. He is our true guide.

I order high and climb a tree. From the glass I contemplate the landscape; the mountains curve slightly to the Northwest. We have to go to the slope on the left and walk, as we did before, within sight of the river.

* * *

Five hours of hard walking has cost us to go to the other slope, but now:

"There it is," I say.

The Chindwin glows in the sunlight. I explore the yellowish stream with my binoculars and see that we will have to be more careful than ever. Through the center, upriver, sails a boat with the flag of the rising sun on the stern mast.

It is certain that there will be patrols around here; There were also them on the other side of the mountain range, if that's what we are going to do. The downside of all this is that I cannot calculate the path that we have traveled all these days. They have been such irregular days in direction and duration that there is no way to translate our effort into miles.

The main precautionary measure is the gurkha, who will serve as a scout. I follow him with the prisoner and the march is closed by Doris.

I am thinking of stopping to eat and rest. It's already after one and it's very hot. I quicken my step to warn the gurkha when he appears, spurred on by an ominous haste.

It surprises me, above all, that he comes so close to me. He brings his mouth close to my ear and says, in a low voice that I barely understand:

"Japanese, sir! A twelve-man patrol.

I look at him questioningly. What is so much mystery about? The gurkha shakes his head.

"That man understands English, sir," he clarifies.

May well be. For the moment you have to hide and be still.

We pick out a thick thicket made up of various kinds of plants and dive into it, pushing our prisoner ahead. Once hidden, we hold its feet and secure the gag, to be sure that it cannot make even the slightest sound.

Furthermore, the gurkha draws his long knife and prepares to nip any attempt to report our presence in the bud.

I see that Doris is very pale. I take her hand and smile, although I'm not as calm as I seem. We have been very lucky so far; the calculation of probabilities says that it cannot last forever. Every step we take north will be more dangerous.

I imagine that we have left some trace and that the Japanese are trying to interpret it in their own way: That assault on the barge and the patrols that we destroyed will have intrigued them.

Because the group of soldiers that we see now differs greatly from the previous ones. They do not walk confidently, chatting happily, as if by a conquered country.

I see them passing there in front, through the hollows of the thicket that hides us. They walk silently, scanning the terrain, spread out in a long line.

I see that some, with their bayonet fixed, are going to get dangerously close to the place that serves as our hiding place. I apprehensively verify that they search the bushes that seem suspicious to them; they get into them, parting the branches with their bayonets. I feel a cold sweat, despite the heat.

If I could find a way to get them away from here, I think; but this is not within my means.

I accidentally put my hand on one of the bags; I hear the buzzing of the furious wasps inside and I feel hope reborn in my chest.

We have three blankets, which we use for camping at night.

"Doris, unfold the blankets! "I order in a whisper." You and the sergeant drop down next to the prisoner and take cover with two of them, leaving no part of his body outside. I'm going to drop one of the swarms.

I help them in the operation. When I see them well covered, I take the remaining blanket and step forward a little to be closer to the small clearing in front of us and through which some Japanese are sniffing.

I cover myself, in turn, and take the bag. Then, carefully, I pull the zipper, taking care that the edges of the zipper do not separate.

I take a look. The terrine has pending. We are on the side of a mountain and the ramp is steep. I wait until the Japanese are closer.

Then I take the satchel by the bottom and shake it energetically, throwing the huge hornet's nest out. I quickly hide my head and hand under the blanket, but I can't avoid a few stings, so I mentally curse all the wasps in the world.

Nothing happens for a few seconds. I'd like to see if the hornet's nest has rolled in the right direction or stopped, hitting some bush.

But it would be crazy. A swarm of wasps is a dangerous thing.

I wait, hearing nothing, until what I expected arrives; a deep and vibrant sound, produced by the wings of hundreds of tropical wasps.

Almost immediately the screams of terror begin among the Japanese soldiers; there is noise of racing, the laments grow in tone and quantity and even shots are fired by those wretches. The wasps are furious after the confinement they have suffered and take their revenge.

Then, quickly, the clamor of the Japanese and the buzz of the wasps are lost in the distance. I lift the blanket a little, checking that there is no danger of Japanese or wasps around.

"Up everyone! "I scream, going out into the clearing." We have to hurry.

My companions, leading the prisoner ahead, join me and we continue the march.

"You are devilishly clever" smiles Doris ". How did you come up with such an idea?

"Remembering an old Kipling book" I reply. In the book, a boy named Mowgli gets rid of his enemies with this trick. I was remembering it this morning when we ran into the hornets' nests.

*　*　*

We have walked all day, with only a half hour break to eat something, at three in the afternoon. It is now seven o'clock and there is little more than an hour until the sun sets.

You have to find a good place to camp. We slow down and look for something that suits us. We are not too lucky. The jungle is very thick around here and we have to stay among the trees.

We suffered a serious setback: the only can opener we had has been lost, loot taken from one of the Japanese patrols. Of course we can continue to open cans with knives, but I was very encouraged to do it in a civilized way.

When we finish dinner we prepare for the night. The prisoner has been behaving well lately, but I distrust him. I would like to discuss something that would free us from his annoying presence, without killing him or letting his freedom mean an additional danger to our presence in these places.

I remember the observation the gurkha made about him. You have some reason to assume that the Japanese understand English. I must stop thinking more about this matter. I already have too many headaches to worry about these minutiae.

The sun is setting. There is a stillness in the environment at this time of day that is very familiar to me. But I don't enjoy it. I think impatience is taking hold of me. It is a bad symptom.

I light a cigarette and go for a walk to calm my nerves. The gurkha is sitting, smoking too, and Doris, who is eating slowly, finishes with her can of Japanese meat.

The prisoner, on the other hand, with his feet tied, but free of hands, has not yet touched hers.

Suddenly he turns to the gurkha and says, in correct English:

"Lend me your knife, please.

That surprises me more than if I had heard a tiger roar. What is yellow hatched in?

I decide not to intervene. The gurkha, without answering, takes his revolver from its holster and then throws his curved knife into it.

I have something like clairvoyance right now. I see clearly that the gurkha believes that he has the solution of this embarrassing company in hand. If the prisoner tries any tricks, he will shoot. But I think the Japanese do not think of hurting us. It has simply reached the limit of its endurance.

Run a finger across the sharp blade to make sure the cut is sharp.

Then, without a moment's hesitation, he thrusts the weapon into his belly and pulls the handle up. Doris screams and goes to where I am.

The gurkha retrieves his knife, cleans it of blood from the Japanese's clothes, and puts it away quietly. For him it is a finished matter.

"We'll get out of here," I suggest. " We still have half an hour of light.

We collect the equipment and leave the corpse of the unfortunate Japanese behind.

"Why will they do these horrible things? Doris asks.

"Hara-kiri" is a national custom, "I explain." It has something to do with honor, but I can't explain exactly why. I think something is wrong inside their heads.

* * *

Four days later, which have passed without incident, they have ushered us a long way, I believe.

We have just set out and it is terribly hot. We are short of water and will have to renew the supply today.

We do it a couple of miles higher, in front of a superb rock formation that blocks our way. There is a small fountain and the water is clear and relatively cool. We drink and fill our canteens, but we don't stop for long. You have to go around the rocky cliffs and continue on your way.

We walked carefully on the lava floor, free of vegetation; it is a relief for the eyes to have clear terrain in front of us. I keep in mind, however, that it is a dangerous path. I want us to get to the jungle as soon as possible, which continues, I suppose, a little further.

We descend the slope and are about to finish the crossing of the rocky passage, when I see something in the distance, below, on the other side of the river.

A city. A relatively large city.

I drop the satchel, and the backpack and light a cigarette, while my companions join me.

"Sittaung in sight" I explain. " I didn't think we would ever make it, but there it is!

Dose looks at me seriously.

"Is the danger over? "question.

"The danger will end when we enter ours; but twenty miles from Sittaung is another town, Tamu, along the border, on the side of the road that leads to Imphal. I don't know if Tamu has fallen to the Japanese; but the front line is there, probably less than a hundred miles from where we are. We have to cross the river as soon as it gets dark. For this we need a means and that is what we are going to look for.

I observe the panorama for a few more moments. Then I propose that we drop all useless weight.

"We will keep the weapons and some cartridges" I expose. " Food for ten days and cigarettes. We will drop everything else.

We lighten up at the moment. It is a shame to leave things that have been so useful to us, but we must conserve strength above all things. This little ground that we have to cover is the most dangerous and all precautions will be few.

We descend the slope quickly until near the river. We do not go out into the open. We slide silently through the jungle, looking for a boat; but there seems to be no chance of finding any, until we spot another native village.

We held a small council of war then.

"Although the natives are friends," I explain, "I think it's prudent for them not to see us.

Some Burmese are on the side of the Japanese "clarifies the Gurkha". My unit was lost mainly because of this cause. Burmese guides were the ones who led the Japanese to meet us.

That decides the question.

"These people have to own boats" I observe "; they'll fish in the river, I guess. We have to locate one and seize it as soon as it gets dark to make the crossing at night.

"I will climb the highest tree I can find, captain," suggests the gurkha. " I'll take your binoculars.

I give them to him and, in a few moments, he climbs like a monkey up the trunk of a jungle giant. It gets lost in the foliage of the glass and we sit under it.

I offer Doris a cigarette and we smoke quietly.

"What is the situation, captain? "asks me.

I look at her smiling.

"I would say that we are friends, Doris" I affirm.

"One of the best" he answers laughing. " What does that have to do with it now?

"You just know that I would like to be called something else other than 'captain'. My friends call me Frank.

"Okay, Frank. Answer my question.

"The situation cannot be better. We have crossed three hundred miles of enemy-occupied territory and are within sight of the goal. We will have difficulties, that's for sure. Over here is the front line. There is a Japanese army, complete, instead of patrols as we have been finding. How we are going to cross that line and get to India is something I do not know completely. But I repeat what I said once: we will get there one way or another. I do know it.

Leaves fall on me and I lift my head. The gurkha is descending. We stand up and wait for him, full of anticipation.

When he reaches the bottom he has a slight smile on his lips.

"There are boats," he says, "on the shore, near the town. It will be easy to get hold of one.

I look triumphantly at Doris. Everything will work out, I feel it inside of me.

VIII

This river crossing is fantastic. We have not encountered difficulties in seizing a boat or in handling it, across the current.

We reached the other shore quickly and left the boat adrift, immediately entering the jungle. It is a short way that we have to do to reach Tamu.

Of all the endless days that we have been crossing the Burmese jungle, today is the most joyful and hopeful because the goal is near.

About two hours later we stop at the top of a hill. There is a small river at our feet and, blinking in the night, a series of luminous points. The lights of Tamu.

The crescent moon barely bathes the landscape, lightening the shadows somewhat. It is enough, however, for us to glimpse the winding strip of a road.

There is movement in it. I attach the binoculars and see that this is very different from the terrain we have left behind. I make out military transport trucks, loaded with material and troops, on their way to the line of fire.

Suddenly the ground in front of us lights up with huge orange flashes, intermittently, and deep roars of artillery reach our ears.

"My God! Doris muses.

I clench my teeth tightly. It is the bulk of the Japanese Army that lies ahead. It would take an insect to pass its lines without being seen. I feel discouraged and, for the first time in all these days, I understand the enormous difficulties of our company.

We sat under a tree and watched the gun battle. The British batteries far away are responding energetically. The howitzers arrive and explode, targeting the Japanese guns. On the other hand, there are air raids.

We cannot see the devices, but they can be heard arriving and dropping their cargo of death in the dark, since Tamu's lights have been turned off. Will the city be in Japanese or British hands?

It seems that a long and bloody battle is taking place at this point. We arrived here in a moment of rest, but now we can see the terrible grandeur of the deadly spectacle.

For my part, I can't understand how we were able to cross the river and get to where we are. From this hill you can see that the region is abuzz with Japanese people. It appears as if the retreating British were holding back the Japanese advance and large masses of Imperial troops were being transported into this sector.

The situation is this: the road is cut ahead. One more step would be to get between the Japanese units. Instead, backtracking, if possible, would be meaningless. Even if it could be done, what the hell were we going to do going back into the Burmese jungle?

I also understand that as soon as daylight breaks we are going to be in mortal danger and I am desperately thinking to find a solution. At least we should do something immediately.

"We are going to recognize this hill" I propose to my companions ". Maybe we'll find a place to hide for a moment.

They take it very seriously. Throughout all this time they have been trusting me, and they continue to do so. The problem will be to remain worthy of this trust.

I imagine my nerves are giving way. As we walk up this hill, I feel that the security that I have had thus far leaves me.

The thoughts running through my brain grow blacker, until Little Gurkha raises his hand and we stop. In front of us, below, on the plain, surrounded by farmland, there is an imposing building for its size.

"A palace," Doris observes.

"A Buddhist monastery," I correct.

The gurkha has a cigarette in his mouth. He hasn't dared to turn it on, however. This is what it is. We can't even smoke quietly.

"We will go to the monastery" I suggest. " We will ask for hospitality and think of something once we are inside.

"Will it be friendly people? Doris's question holds great significance.

"We will know when we go," I answer decisively.

We left the hill and approached the monastery, constantly fearing to run into a Japanese patrol. This does not happen; We arrived at the huge, nailed door and I knocked, hitting the wood with the butt of the submachine gun.

The sound is hollow, impressive. We waited for several minutes, filled with an anxiety that we tried to hide. It could be the case that it is empty. Or serve as accommodation to a Japanese unit.

A window in the door opens and an Asian face looks at us without the slightest sign of astonishment.

I have an idea at that precise moment. I pull my wallet out of my pocket and pull out a business card. It says: "Frank Latimer, Aeronautical Engineer, New York, N.Y." A peacetime card. I give it to the doorman (I suppose it will be), and the window closes again.

After another tense wait, the door creaks, and begins to open. We are admitted!

We enter. I'm already seeing things with more optimism, a little prematurely, no doubt.

The door closes again. This is pitch dark.

The voice of the man who has admitted us sounds for the first time, in very faulty English.

"The monastery is a place of peace," he says. They must leave their weapons here.

It may be a trap. Perhaps the Japanese want us to capture without having to fight. But, despite everything, I have confidence in these Buddhists, people who are not even authorized by their religion to kill a bird.

"What do you think, Doris? "I ask.

"I can't advise, Frankie" he replies.

"You, Sergeant?

"The decision is not mine" is a polite but firm answer.

"Well, we will lay down our weapons" I decide.

We detach ourselves from them, knives included, and start walking behind our guide. We climb some stone stairs and go through endless corridors.

Finally, the guide stops before an open door. A faint light comes out from inside the room.

"They can happen" he tells us.

He bows and silently disappears down the corridor.

I shrug. I take Doris by the arm and we enter, followed by the brave gurkha.

The room is wide, with bare walls, with a carpet in the center, on which there is a man seated in the oriental style. Lighting is provided by a simple candle, burning in a simple metal candelabrum.

"Welcome back" this man's English is perfect. " Please take a seat.

We sat across from him. We hope you tell us more.

"I am the head of this community," he continues. You seek hospitality and I offer it to you, but I cannot assure you. So far, the Japanese have not bothered us. However, things can vary. In other words, it will not be healthy for you or us to stay here indefinitely.

I nod.

"I understand" I admit. " I thank you, anyway. Can you provide us with some reports?

Ask, sir.

"How far are the British lines?"

"About fifteen miles yesterday.

"What chance would we have of reaching them?

Shake your head negatively.

"Come on, none. There are thousands of Japanese "he explains.

"Walking? "I ask, intrigued." How else could you try?

The Buddhist monk stares at me, somewhat puzzled.

"Flying" he says.

"But we don't have a plane.

"Do it yourself" is the surprising invitation.

"Make a plane? "I say it with the astonishment reflected on my features.

It's like being asked to lay an egg.

"You are an aeronautical engineer. Your card says so. The Wright brothers were not. They wanted to fly, then they made an airplane and they flew. I think that is a logical suggestion.

Why not? Maybe it could be tried, but... there are too many impossible things in such a plan. The bad thing about it is that Doris and the gurkha are looking at me with an expression that I don't like. It seems as if they believe that I can solve everything.

"We would need a powerful engine," he indicated.

"It is not impossible to get one" smiles the monk.

"Later, you would need tools.

"Maybe we can lend you some.

"What about cloth, glue, wires, gasoline, a place to work and another to take off from?

"It is possible, everything is possible as long as it is desired with sufficient intensity" smiles the monk.

To wish?

"Our most fervent aspiration is to reach the British lines, that is the truest thing there is under the sun," he replied heatedly.

"Then" our host tells us, "they will get it. Tomorrow we will talk more calmly about all this. Now, rest.

He stands up and bows to us. He disappears silently, closing the door when leaving the room.

"Good" says Doris ", now that everything is settled, I think I am going to sleep peacefully for the first time in a long time.

I'm about to groan. What is solved? Where is the plane that is going to take us away from here? How am I going to build it and with what?

I don't seem to go to sleep, at least not easily.

* * *

The head of the Buddhist monastic community seems convinced that everything is going smoothly. He has led me to the great courtyard. It is enormously long, more than six hundred yards, I reckon.

"They can take off from here. The walls, which are barely six feet high, will not be an obstacle, "he explains.

Perfect, but what are we going to take off with?

Then he takes me to a very wide door that opens onto the patio. He locks it up and shows me something I didn't expect to find. It is a car, an old-fashioned 'Rolls', but apparently well preserved.

"The engine and many usable parts" smiles my companion.

I climb into the car and start it. The engine runs, at least. With the wheels, a landing gear could be made and there are quite a few bolts and accessories in the rest of the body that would do the trick.

"At that table" continues my kind guest, "there is paper for you to do your calculations. I leave you alone, Mr. Latimer.

He leaves and I start to think. This is a crazy company. Assuming you are able to build the airplane, you will have to jump into the air without testing it. And at night, too. How am I going to fly at night without instruments? Above all, will I be able to build anything that can fly?

I sit at the small table, take my calculating ruler out of my pocket, and begin to work on the plan. It will have to be a simple device, a monoplane similar to those that began to cross the skies, very low, by the way, at the beginning of the century.

Of all the early model aircraft that I could remember, I chose the "Bleriot XI"; it was the first aircraft with which the French flew in the war of fourteen, a classic of the air. Rectilinear, with a square wooden frame and covered in fabric, it seemed the best that could be attempted in the current circumstances.

But there was a terrible obstacle. The weight of the engine of the «Rolls» and that of an axle and two wheels of the car could never be elevated in the air by such a device.

Then it occurred to me that I could do without the wheels. I would build a kind of sled skates that would help me land. The wheels would not be attached to the device, but it would rest on them. A couple of holes in the skates and axle, with a loose pin, would do the trick. When raised, the apparatus would ground the wheels.

You have to get to work seriously. I leave the "Rolls" and go to make things concrete with my colleagues. Doris and the gurkha will be my assistants and it will be necessary to see if they will bring me the wires, the cloth and the wood that I need.

* * *

There is not much time to waste. The British are backing down. I know that the Japanese advance will end one of these days and that the Allies will make them flee in the direction of Tokyo, but this belongs to the future. At the moment, don't expect to fly a lot with the thing I'm building.

I am informed that the British lines are already some forty miles from Tamu. It's already quite a distance.

It is the construction of the ailerons and elevator and rudders that gives me the most work. The wires that have been provided to me at the monastery come from very different origins and are not to be trusted.

Instead, the wood of the frames has been replaced, with advantage I think, by bamboo, stronger and easier to assemble.

I look at Doris.

"This is going" I say.

"I'll believe it when I see it" he smiles. Will "this" really fly?

I laugh, a little forced, and nod.

"I wouldn't be the least bit surprised," I admit. "

The gurkha, on the other hand, is proving to be a skilled worker; quickly understands what is being said and has good hands.

He does not express his doubts. Maybe it doesn't have any. If I say the artifact will fly, take it for granted.

The structure is almost finished. The fabric has received a layer of glue that will serve as a varnish, to give it consistency and prevent breakage.

I am busy making the propeller. It is delicate work, but according to my calculations, it will have to work well. From wood, too, I have made a pulley. I have adapted it to the fan shaft to give it a larger diameter. Thus it will multiply the rotations by transmitting them, by means of a belt, to the propeller shaft, also my work, taken from a bearing that I have been able to cut after tearing it off.

We work in a hurry. We know that this situation cannot last. There are more and more Japanese around here, and even if he hasn't told me, I know that the generous head of the monastery is concerned. If we are discovered, the end of the community is certain.

That is why we have taken advantage of these days from dawn to night. Really, all the important work is on the roof. It only remains to assemble the motor. Gasoline there are almost a hundred liters, stored in cans, enough and much more to make a short trip.

Will this monster fly? That is what I constantly ask myself, as the construction of the apparatus progresses.

The head of the community meets us. His name is Mingim and he is a man of considerable culture.

He stares at our work admiringly.

"Wonderful," he exclaims.

I look at the device again. It's a horrible thing, some kind of prehistoric pterodactyl, bat-winged and ugly as a devil.

"They will have to hurry" continues our friend.

I feel something akin to fear.

"What news is there? I ask him.

"The British are about a hundred miles away," he replies, smiling. " But I have received a visit from some Japanese officers. More are ordered to house a general with his staff. It is impossible for me to refuse.

"When will those gentlemen come? "I want to know.

"Tomorrow night.

"I understand" he replied. Tonight will be the moment.

Doris looks at me thoughtfully and the gurkha stops working, waiting to hear something else.

"I'm afraid you don't have more time, Captain" smiles Mingim.

I look at my watch. It's three o'clock. We will have to take advantage of all the light of the day to assemble the engine, about five or six hours.

"Good" I smile, making an effort ", the flight will be today. The moon won't rise until twelve thirty at night. Then we will take off.

We go to work with feverish activity. We have been through too many hardships and suffered too many fears for everything to disappear now when we almost touch freedom with our hands.

We assembled the engine, in which operation I use all the screws that I had left after disassembling a large part of the Rolls. I hope you can hold the machine in place despite the vibrations.

Before sunset, the work is finished. We took the plane out of the garage, for which the door had to be widened, knocking down part of the wall.

We put it in the garden, a vast expanse of land with only one tree in one corner. This is so so as not to distract the walking monks from their meditations.

It's already dark. We will have to wait until twelve thirty. When the moon rises I hope to be able to maintain eye contact with the earth, as we will fly low.

I examine the horizon in the direction that we shall follow. You will have to use the valleys between mountains to get more than a hundred miles away from here. Actually, I intend to fly as much as possible, to be sure not to fall into the Japanese lines.

You have to rest now. Eat something, prepare for the greatest adventure of our lives. Let's go fly in a homemade airplane! This is enough to scare anyone and, above all, me, who has built and planned it and I know the many limitations it must have and how little we can trust the materials we have used.

*　*　*

The moon is already in the sky. Her pale face has risen above the mountains behind us. There is enough clarity, an essential condition to be able to fly at night without instruments.

The cockpit has a bench-shaped seat, in which the three of us will ride, my two companions on horseback, who will occupy the rear. Seat belts with ropes, tied to our waists and then to the bench, which, on the other hand, I do not know if it will have enough resistance to support our weight if the air made us turn around.

We do not carry luggage, not even weapons. Losing weight is essential; that's why the starter motor and batteries were left out. We say goodbye to Mingim, one of the few people we have seen in here. The other monks have not wanted to disturb their spirits by dealing with us.

It's a short, but excited farewell. This man has made our escape possible when we no longer had any hope.

"I hope we will see each other again" I smile as I shake his hand.

"I hope so too" he tells me. I wish you luck.

The oriental who serves as a gatekeeper to the community turns the propeller, just as I instructed him. The engine starts without incident. I wait for it to warm up. I maneuver with the control pedals and with the lever, rough works of bamboo and wire. They seem to work in order.

I wave and turn to my companions.

"Let's take off! "I tell you". Fingers crossed ... and keep it that way until we get there.

I accelerate and the plane begins to glide across the garden, picking up speed. According to my calculations, we will take off at sixty miles per hour, and eighty or ninety will be the most we can go.

I throttle to the top, staring at the walls in front of us. The moon lights them up very well. Second after second we gain speed and we approach them. With the consequent alarm I realize that the wings do not seem to take in enough air. We may very well crash against that wall.

I pull the joystick back. Nothing happens for a couple of seconds. The wheels, although the axle is loose, can exert such pressure, due to the speed, that the system will allow me to lift myself even if they do not work.

Suddenly, the apparatus rises and we pass over the threatening wall. We're flying!

Joy floods my soul, but I don't let this feeling get me intoxicated. We can fly, but it will be a very short time. The consistent grease, taken from the gearbox of the «Rolls», will not be able to resist too much on the propeller shaft, when it is heated by the rotation.

With every minute that passes I realize how difficult it is to handle the monster I pilot. They do not obey the commands except grudgingly and growling. I wonder if my arms and legs are not going to tire too quickly, due to the enormous traction I have to exert to handle them.

Instead, the flight conditions are magnificent. We are only going a few hundred feet up. The ground, the black treetops and the roofs of many houses and cabins are perfectly visible.

I can even make out some Japanese drums. I hope they open fire on us, but the Japanese anti-aircraft guns fail to do so.

I imagine, with a smile, the surprise they will have down there when they see us and, above all, when they hear us. There is no airplane in the world that sounds the same. It will baffle them, for sure. This is not a fast and modern airplane, therefore they will refrain from firing at us for fear of being wrong.

My arms are heavy like lead. This is not flying an airplane, but fighting it. I head a valley between two mountains, always to the west, and we raise the echoes of the night. There is a truce, apparently, between the combatants down there. We don't see cannons firing or any kind of warlike activity.

Something is starting to splatter on my face. The smell of gasoline reaches my nose. The tank, one of the tanks of the «Rolls», I have mounted on the hood of the device. It must have some escape. And it means two things, mainly. That we can lose a lot of gas and be forced to make a hard landing, for one thing. On the other hand, it indicates that there is imminent danger that we will catch fire.

The wind hits my face so violently that the eyes water profusely. I have a terrible job keeping them open. We leave the valley and I glance briefly at my watch. In the moonlight I can do it.

It's almost two o'clock. We must have traveled about two hundred miles, more than enough to be on the British lines. On the other hand, I fear that this thing will disintegrate, and it is becoming more and more difficult for me to control it.

Landing is imposed. We have done what we can. It would be a horrible thing to die now, when we have earned our freedom after so many hardships.

I scan the ground. It seems that we have a regularly flat stretch free of vegetation; But, in this low light, I can't be sure.

However, I decide to give it a try. I descend slowly and when I describe a circle and see the land against the light, I make out the shimmering of the moon on the water. Rice fields! The best, in the absence of an airfield.

"We landed, we landed! "I yell at my teammates.

I don't think they heard me, but my hand gestures speak volumes.

The ground is fast approaching. I slow down and operate the joystick as smoothly as I can.

At first contact, water and mud fly through the air, splashing us, but that does not matter. All over the paddy field again and the sled-style skates glide perfectly. It is a magnificent landing, considering the circumstances, albeit with an unexpected, unpredictable ending.

The terrace abruptly ends below us and the idea flashes through my brain that the next one is much lower.

We fall heavily and freeze, finally. The shock has been tremendous. I feel a sharp pain in my right leg.

My companions seem unharmed. Between the two of them they take me out of the cockpit and we splash around in the middle of the rice paddy. But I can't walk. That damn leg must be broken.

Just then things start to happen. Nearby engines are heard, there are headlights that illuminate us and voices are heard.

But, thank God they be given! Those voices scream in English.

The first ones who arrive with us do not know what side to take, whether to take care of our people or contemplate the strange artifact that has taken us there.

"Where did you get it from, friends? Asks a Scottish lieutenant, judging by the accent.

"They are survivors of the First World War" explains a funny man.

"It must be a rare model of broom" explains a third. Sorcerers and witches are also modernizing.

Finally, we are transferred in an ambulance and on the way, we find out that we are near Imphal. We haven't even done a hundred miles; the head wind, very strong, barely let us advance, but we are now safe.

At Imphal we part ways. I go to a hospital and Doris and the gurkha are captured for questioning by the British Intelligence Service.

The leg is broken, but it is not serious. Forty days in a cast and in circulation again.

The bad thing is that the Intelligence boys come to visit me. There is one of them, Colonel Graduation, who makes me repeat the details of our escape from Burma over and over again. He never ceases to say, "Really?" Impressive! Amazing!"

Then I can talk to my fellow escapees. Doris is more wonderfully pretty than ever. He tells me that he has already had six marriage proposals.

That puts me in a bad mood.

"I think mine should take precedence," I put out sullenly.

"It's what I think" smiles Doris.

I'm very tired. I want to sleep, sleep a dozen years, but this is important.

"I also thought that Little Gurkha should be our godfather" I explain.

"I would have requested it," says Doris; if you hadn't proposed it yourself.

* * *

This is Yunnan, China. Many things have "happened since I left America willing to join the group of" Flying Tigers "; but, like almost everything I set my mind to, I have succeeded. I am here, despite everything, ready to fly with this famous unit.

In Madras there is a nice "bungalow" where Doris will be waiting for me. We got married a month ago, when I got out of the hospital, and we already know a lot about each other.

On the other hand, I will add one more fact: Little Gurkha was, of course, our best man. So I found out his name. The brave sergeant from my Burmese days, now a lieutenant, is called "really" Rashmon Benagar.

Precisely today I had a letter from both of you. Doris tells me that she is fine, but that I must ask permission the first time, as she is very lonely. Rashmon, on the other hand, longs for those days of our epic.

"There is a lot of movement on the Burma front," he tells me, but it is all very different, Captain. I think we had a better time then. Above all, that magnificent flight, in your apparatus, I will not forget as long as I live.

For my part, I prefer to fly in one of these modern devices.

Although, after all, I think Rashmon is right. Those Burmese days weren't so bad.

But this belongs to the past. Now to fight.

END